"Who hurt you, C...

"One of my patients got upset. It's nothing, Mark."

"The hell it's not. A patient attacked you and you call it nothing?"

"He reacted to a traumatic memory and I happened to get in the way. It goes with the territory." She pulled away, but he caught her arm, refusing to let her run.

"His name, Claire?"

She shook her head. "I can't tell you that, Mark."

"Can't or won't?"

"Both. If I don't protect my patients' privacy, they won't confide in me. Then I'm useless."

"And how helpful will you be to your patients if you end up dead?"

He wrapped his arms around her, determined to make her realize she might be in danger. "You can't trust anyone, Claire. Not right now. It's too dangerous."

"I know how dangerous trusting a man can be, Mark. After all, I once trusted you."

Dear Harlequin Intrigue Reader,

August marks a special month at Harlequin Intrigue as we commemorate our twentieth anniversary! Over the past two decades we've satisfied our devoted readers' diverse appetites with a vast smorgasbord of romantic suspense page-turners. Now, as we look forward to the future, we continue to stand by our promise to deliver thrilling mysteries penned by stellar authors.

As part of our celebration, our much-anticipated new promotion, ECLIPSE, takes flight. With one book planned per month, these stirring Gothic-inspired stories will sweep you into an entrancing landscape of danger, deceit…and desire. Leona Karr sets the stage for mind-bending mystery with debut title, *A Dangerous Inheritance*.

A high-risk undercover assignment turns treacherous when smoldering seduction turns to forbidden love, in *Bulletproof Billionaire* by Mallory Kane, the second installment of NEW ORLEANS CONFIDENTIAL. Then, peril closes in on two torn-apart lovers, in *Midnight Disclosures*— Rita Herron's latest book in her spine-tingling medical research series, NIGHTHAWK ISLAND.

Patricia Rosemoor proves that the fear of the unknown can be a real aphrodisiac in *On the List*—the fourth installment of CLUB UNDERCOVER. Code blue! Patients are mysteriously dropping like flies in Boston General Hospital, and it's a race against time to prevent the killer from striking again, in *Intensive Care* by Jessica Andersen.

To round off an unforgettable month, Jackie Manning returns to the lineup with *Sudden Alliance*—a woman-in-jeopardy tale fraught with nonstop action…and a lethal attraction!

Join in on the festivities by checking out all our selections this month!

Sincerely,

Denise O'Sullivan
Harlequin Intrigue Senior Editor

MIDNIGHT
DISCLOSURES
1-2-5

RITA HERRON

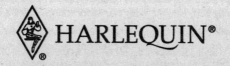

HARLEQUIN®

TORONTO • NEW YORK • LONDON
AMSTERDAM • PARIS • SYDNEY • HAMBURG
STOCKHOLM • ATHENS • TOKYO • MILAN • MADRID
PRAGUE • WARSAW • BUDAPEST • AUCKLAND

ISBN 0-373-22790-6

MIDNIGHT DISCLOSURES

This edition published by arrangement with Harlequin Books S.A.

® and TM are trademarks of the publisher. Trademarks indicated with ® are registered in the United States Patent and Trademark Office, the Canadian Trade Marks Office and in other countries.

www.eHarlequin.com

Printed in U.S.A.

ABOUT THE AUTHOR

Award-winning author Rita Herron wrote her first book when she was twelve, but didn't think real people grew up to be writers. Now she writes so she doesn't have to get a *real* job. A former kindergarten teacher and workshop leader, she traded her storytelling for kids for romance, and writes romantic comedies and romantic suspense. She lives in Georgia with her own romance hero and three kids. She loves to hear from readers so please write her at P.O. Box 921225, Norcross, GA 30092-1225, or visit her Web site at www.ritaherron.com.

Books by Rita Herron

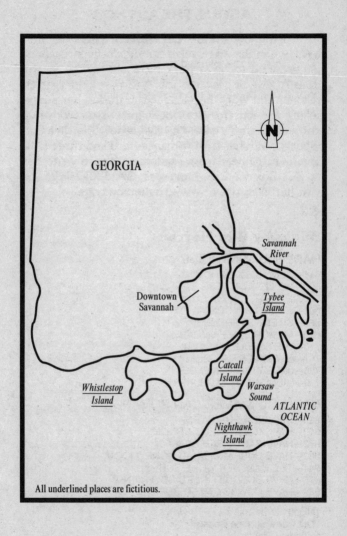

GEORGIA

Savannah
River

Downtown
Savannah

Tybee
Island

Catcall
Island

Warsaw
Sound

Whistlestop
Island

ATLANTIC
OCEAN

Nighthawk
Island

All underlined places are fictitious.

CAST OF CHARACTERS

Dr. Claire Kos—Blinded by the accident that cost her her child, Claire Kos has nothing to live for but work. Will that very job cost her her life?

Mark Steele—A man struggling with guilt and loss. Can he save Claire before a ruthless serial killer makes her his next victim?

Special Agent Luke Devlin—An FBI agent with demons of his own, he offers Mark a job when Mark has nothing left. But will that job be Mark's salvation or his downfall?

Dr. Ian Hall—The new director of the Coastal Island Research Park wants to create positive publicity for CIRP. But is his plan a smoke screen to hide secretive research under way at the center?

Dr. George Ferguson and Dr. Kurt Lassiter—Two of Claire's co-workers who lust after her. Would one of them kill to have her?

Drew Myers—The man who created the idea of the *Calling Claire* show. Just how far will he go to make the show a success?

Joel Sanger—A psychotic patient of Claire's with violent tendencies toward women. Has he become a serial killer?

Richard Wheaton—Another patient suffering from dissociative identity disorder. Is one of his personalities a murderer?

Al Hogan—A troubled man who attended a support group with Claire months ago and tried to befriend her. Has he resurfaced?

To my cool aunt Nelda—
who finally got hooked on romance!
Love, Rita

Prologue

She had to tell Mark about the baby.

Claire Kos punched the accelerator, flipped on the windshield wipers and wove her way through the late-evening traffic. Mark couldn't leave on some dangerous mission without knowing she planned to accept his proposal, that she'd be waiting for him when he returned.

She understood his need to serve his country. He'd been raised by a military father, had grown up on a base himself. He'd been born and bred for the armed services, a true hero. His reasons were all very noble.

And she knew she was being selfish. But what about her and their unborn child? What would happen to them if he didn't return?

Telling him won't keep him from leaving.

She gripped the tiny silver frame she'd bought as a going-away gift in her hand. He could take the frame with him, and if he couldn't make it back for the birth, she'd mail him a photograph to put inside. That way she and their child would always be with him, wherever he went.

Thunder clapped in the gray sky, the rain rushing down in a torrent, the shadows of the night closing in around her. A hurricane warning had been issued on the coast of Florida, the torrential rains already unleashing themselves on Atlanta.

Reminding herself that she had another life to consider now, a baby to protect, she eased her foot off the accelerator, but another pair of headlights behind her, set on high beam, nearly blinded her. She blinked and righted the wheel to correct for the curve in the road, but a horn blared as an oncoming truck roared toward her. She skimmed the edge of the embankment, spotted the bridge ahead and panic slammed into her.

Behind her another car honked, speeding up on her tail. She skidded on the wet pavement, her Jetta hurling into a tailspin. The passenger side scraped the side rails of the bridge and sparks flew from the car as it careened down the riverbank, grinding over the muddy earth. Glass exploded as she nosedived into the Chattahoochee River.

The air bag exploded, trapping her against the seat. Spots danced before her eyes, and panic knifed through her arms as a stabbing pain shot through her temple.

She had to save the baby.

Water seeped into the car, the current lapping at the windows. She jiggled the seat belt to escape, pushing at the air bag, but the seat belt was stuck. Red water swirled around her.

Blood.

Her stomach cramped, a spasm of mind-numbing agony gripping her. She cried out, tears running from her eyes. The red faded into black. Then darkness. She reached for the tiny picture frame and clutched it in her hand.

Dear God. No. She was losing her baby. They would both die. And Mark would leave the country without ever knowing that she'd planned to accept his proposal.

Or that she had been pregnant with his child.

Chapter One

A year later

Claire Kos lived in a world of darkness—a world she'd been trying to adjust to since the day she'd lost her child.

Feeling her way to her desk, she slid into the chair, adjusted the microphone and tried to banish thoughts of her own personal problems. So far, *Calling Claire*, as her radio talk show had been dubbed, had been a major hit in Savannah. Her callers consisted of people who wanted to discuss love gone wrong, divorces, depression, family and parental issues.

Ironic that she should be offering advice on love when her own relationship had self-destructed.

She heard noise on the other side of the glass window and sensed the producer, Drew Myers, gearing up for the show. Drew handled a hundred things at once, all deftly, as well as screening incoming calls. The station had worked out a system so he could signal her with a buzzer.

As a concession to Claire's concern for the potential threats to herself and the show, and out of concern for the callers, she and the station manager had agreed to keep the topics on a fairly light note, hoping to avoid any issues which might need a more thorough professional assessment.

She checked her braille watch, then laid her hand over the buzzer. The familiar ding alerted her to begin the show.

The first caller complained of a cheating husband, which prompted several callers to admit their own spouse's extramarital affair. The last caller hit a nerve—her husband had abandoned her and their infant son.

She thought of Mark.

Not that Mark had really abandoned her. He'd gone off to war, while she'd fought a war of her own at home.

Sometimes she wondered if she should have informed him of her accident. Other times, she assured herself she'd been right not to burden him with her problems. Besides, he hadn't exactly contacted her after he'd left.

A signal alerted her to the next caller. "Hello, this is Claire, how can I help you?"

"I… I can't s-see," a woman cried. "It's so dark. P-please help me."

Claire froze, the desperation in the woman's high-pitched voice sending a chill down her spine.

"Tell me your name," she said softly. "Where are you?"

Instead of the woman's voice, a muffled voice began to sing, "Blinded by the light…"

A chill skated up Claire's spine. "Who is this? Is this some kind of sick joke?" She jerked her head up, wishing she could see Drew's reaction, then motioned for him to trace the call, another stipulation she'd insisted upon before signing on with the program. She had no intention of offering free advice to spike ratings in lieu of true professional care.

"She was a bad girl, a very bad girl, Claire," the muffled voice whispered. "Do you know what happens to bad girls?"

Claire struggled to detect the sounds in the background, anything that might offer her a clue as to the woman's location. The wind howled. Some kind of bird cawed. She heard the ocean waves crashing against the shore. The man was outside, using a cell phone.

It would be harder to trace.

"Tell me who this is," she whispered. "Let me speak to the woman again."

"It's too late for her," the dark voice murmured. "But save yourself, Claire. Goodbye."

Then the phone went dead, the woman's cry for help fading into an eerie silence. Panic bolted through Claire.

Had she just been talking to a killer?

A week later

LIEUTENANT MARK STEELE had once lived for the military.

Unfortunately, his last army mission had gone awry, and five of his men had been killed. Although Mark had lived, he'd been injured and had spent time in an enemy prison camp. But not before he'd shot the traitor who'd revealed his men's location.

He'd thought that bit of justice might assuage the guilt that had eaten away at him ever since, but it hadn't even nibbled at the edges. Blinking against the blinding noonday sun, he entered the Atlanta Federal office building. Since he'd accepted a medical discharge, he'd been slogging through every day, searching for a reason to get up every morning. This new job, tracking down criminals, even if they were civilians, might give him a renewed purpose in life. God knew he needed it.

A fair-haired man in a dark suit and tie greeted him, although the normally arrogant attitude he'd always associated with the feds was absent, a dark soulless look haunting the man's eyes. Mark instantly connected. He'd witnessed the same desolation in soldiers' eyes just before they died.

"Luke Devlin," the man said without preamble. He gestured toward two other agents seated at the table and introduced them.

"It's nice to have you on board, Mr. Steele."

Mark nodded, still adjusting to civilian life. "Thanks. I'm anxious for an assignment." Anything to take his mind off the lost men. His lost career.

His lost love, Claire.

"We're organizing a special task force to investigate certain aspects of government intelligence as well as the Coastal Island Research Park's work on Nighthawk Island. Are you familiar with the research center?"

"I've read about the facility. It's in Savannah?"

"Right." Devlin moved to the wall, gestured toward a detailed map of the research islands, then quickly reviewed recent events at the center.

"There's been trouble at CIRP, unethical research taking place. And Arnold Hughes, the first director and founder of the research center, actually had a scientist killed because he discovered Hughes wanted to sell his research to the highest bidder," Devlin said. "Hughes escaped our first attempt to catch him, then reappeared with a new identity, but the local police have recently arrested him."

Mark nodded.

"The new director, Ian Hall, appears to be trying to change CIRP's reputation, but we have reason to believe there are some high-level secret projects taking place. Some have government clearance, others…we'd like to see stopped."

"Interesting. Go on."

"In conjunction with Ian Hall's good faith publicity, a psychologist named Dr. Claire Kos recently began hosting a radio talk show in Savannah. You know Dr. Kos, don't you?"

"Yes." His heart pounded. An image of Claire Kos's beautiful honey-blond hair floated through his mind like a summer breeze. God, he'd been so in love with her.

But she hadn't even bothered to come to the airport to say goodbye. He'd waited like a fool until the last minute, hoping she'd show and accept his proposal.

Two weeks later, he'd received his engagement ring in the mail. Still, he'd hoped she would change her mind.

But six months had passed with no word, then six more. She had obviously moved on with her life. Not that he could blame her. After all, she must have decided she couldn't handle the military life just as his own mother had.

He glanced down at the floor and in his mind, saw the bloody corpses of his fellow soldiers.

Better she had moved on.

She hadn't understood his compulsion to do his job. To live up to the standards of his military father, a war hero in his own right. What would the colonel say if he could see his son today?

"You don't suspect Claire of being involved in an unethical project?"

Devlin shrugged. "There is talk about research using hypnosis as well as mind-altering drugs that have been used before to brainwash people. By cozying up to Dr. Kos, we're hoping you can explore that issue, among others."

He stiffened. So that's the reason they were assigning him to this mission. They wanted him to use Claire? "I can assure you Claire isn't involved. She's one of the most noble, dedicated doctors I've ever known." Besides being the most beautiful and loving. But after all he'd seen in the past few years, he was too empty inside to have anything to offer a woman. And he couldn't forgive Claire for not being there when he needed her most.

She wouldn't be very proud of the man he was now, either.

"But she can help you gain access to the center," Devlin said.

Mark opened his mouth to protest, then clamped it shut. He'd never allowed personal feelings to interfere with his job. He wouldn't now.

Devlin cleared his throat. "There's a new development, though, that takes precedence. In the past two weeks Dr. Kos has received phone calls on her radio talk show from two different women who were abducted. Later, police found both women's bodies."

"They were murdered?"

"Yes. The locals suspect a serial killer, so they've officially called us in." Devlin punched a recording, and Mark went completely cold inside as he listened to the chilling calls.

Save yourself, Claire.

What the hell had the killer meant? Was he threatening Claire?

CLAIRE'S HANDS trembled as she headed to the door. It would probably be the police again with more questions. Questions she didn't have the answers to.

She massaged her neck, rubbing away the tension. After that horrifying phone call the night before, she hadn't slept a wink. She'd also rescheduled her patient load for the day.

How could she help others when she'd failed the women who'd phoned in needing her help? Even though she wasn't directly responsible, their deaths weighed heavily on Claire's conscience.

She bumped into the wall, the sharp edge digging into her hip as she reached for the doorknob. Measuring her steps always grew more difficult when her emotions were involved, or if she was tired. She pressed the call button. "Who's there?"

"FBI, Dr. Kos, Special Agent Luke Devlin and Agent Steele, we need to ask you some questions."

Steele? This had to be a coincidence. Someone with the same last name, that's all. Mark was overseas, not FBI.

And what could she tell them that she hadn't told the cops?

"Just a moment." She unlocked the door, leaving the chain intact. "Do you have identification?"

Clothing rustled as the man removed something from his pocket. She accepted the ID through the crack in the door. Holding the badge in front of her as if she could still see it, she slid her fingers over the edges, studying it for authenticity, well aware how limited she'd become without her sight. How could she determine if it was a forgery?

Vaguely satisfied the man was who he claimed to be, she unchained the door and stepped aside.

"Thank you, Dr. Kos." Luke Devlin's voice sounded strained, tired, like a man doing an unpleasant job.

Then a whiff of a dark masculine scent mingled with a woodsy smell wafted upward and she froze. No, it couldn't be…

"HELLO, CLAIRE."

Panic jammed the words in her throat. "Mark? What are you doing here?"

"I work for the government now," he said in a husky voice.

But why? Mark had been so committed to the military.

"Dr. Kos, do you mind if we come in and sit down?" Agent Devlin asked.

Claire was so shaken her body temporarily went into lockdown. Her first instinct was to tell them to leave, to take Mark and his intoxicating scent and his big masculine presence away. But her voice refused to work, and her legs threatened to collapse beneath her, so she gestured toward the living area.

"Certainly." She turned and stumbled, then paused to reorient herself. Agent Devlin's hard soles clattered on the wooden floor as he stepped inside, but Mark remained in the doorway as if he didn't want to reenter the graveyard of their shattered relationship.

"Claire." His throaty voice echoed with emotions she couldn't quite name. Shock. Anger. Bewilderment.

"Come in." She forced herself not to react to his voice, but he caught her arm and swung her around. Cupping her face in his hands, he tilted her head toward him. She released a shaky breath, and blinked to focus, aching to see him. She imagined his strong jaw covered in five o'clock shadow, his neatly clipped black hair, the small cleft in his chin, his broad nose and that tight military air. And then those big hands all over her, touching her, exploring, making her his, his guarded look fading, his eyes darkening with passion....

One reason she hadn't phoned him after the accident. She'd wanted him so badly it was scary. But she had to learn to stand alone.

He ran his hands over her face, and she blinked, forcing back tears.

"God, Claire," he croaked. "What the hell happened to you?"

Chapter Two

Claire's heart pounded in her chest. How could she answer him without confiding everything. He couldn't know...

"Claire, talk to me. What happened?" Raw shock hardened his voice.

"I had an accident. Now let me go, Mark, and let's sit down."

Instead of releasing her, his grip tightened. "What kind of accident?"

"A car accident."

Still hanging on to her, his breath brushed her cheek, eliciting memories of a hot night between the sheets, their bodies moving together in a heated rhythm of passion that had left her aching for more.

Forever.

But that would never be. Not now.

Agent Devlin cleared his throat. "Steele, the case, our questions?"

She heard Mark's feet snap together, imagined him standing rigid with anger. She knew him well enough to recognize that the ironclad control on his emotions had been shaken, and he was wrestling to regain his equilibrium.

But erotic visions interceded into the darkness where she lived, resurrecting a longing for the past—the coarse stiffness of his short hair brushing her belly, his lips tracing a path along the curve of her spine.

And his eyes—she'd never seen a man with eyes his color. They were almost golden, rimmed in pale yellow. Filled with passion, they turned almost chocolate-brown, with laughter, the gold shimmered like sunshine.

Although he'd hardly ever laughed.

She'd wanted him to laugh more, had tried to ease the hardness in his eyes, take away the loneliness.

Now she'd forgotten how to laugh herself.

"Sit down," Claire implored softly. "I'll get us some coffee and we'll talk."

His labored sigh heightened the tension between them, but he finally dropped his hands. "Fine."

Claire turned, so desperate to reorient herself that she ignored his clipped tone. The last thing she wanted was to make a fool of herself or give the image that she was helpless.

She did not want Mark's pity.

Another reason she hadn't informed him of her accident or condition. She'd been smothered enough by her sister Paulette's well-meaning intentions.

She recounted her steps to the den, thankfully bypassing the furniture without a bump. It was imperative that her belongings stay in place. If a table or stool were moved, she'd trip and fall on her face.

Something she absolutely could not do in front of a strong man like Mark.

"Have a seat, gentlemen, and I'll get some coffee."

"I'll help." Mark moved up behind her.

"No, I can handle it." She didn't bother to apologize for her own abrupt tone. She needed time to compose herself before facing Mark again.

The current situation with the women who'd been murdered had already destroyed her peace of mind.

She slipped into the kitchen nook, removed a serving tray, stacked three cups on it along with the coffee-pot which she kept filled all day, then added sugar and creamer and returned to the den. Her hands trembled as she set it on the coffee table.

"Please serve yourselves, gentlemen."

"Thanks, Dr. Kos," Agent Devlin said from the big armchair.

"Sit down, Claire." Mark's voice came from the love seat.

She poured herself a cup of coffee, using two fingers to measure, then slid onto the sofa, feeling his scruti-nizing eyes trace her every movement.

"When did you have this accident?" Mark asked.

An involuntary shudder passed through her. This was the question she'd dreaded most. *The night you left*, she wanted to scream. *I was rushing to the airport to accept your proposal, to tell you about our baby.*

Now, he would never know. He *couldn't* know.

"A few months ago. I'm fine now."

"You're not fine, you're blind," Mark said in a gruff voice.

"That's true," Claire conceded, "but thanks to the wonderful rehab program at CIRP, I'm learning to adjust." She crossed her legs, determined to change the subject. "Now, Agent Devlin, why is Lieutenant Steele with you? Do you have news about the two women who were murdered?"

Claire tightened her hands around her coffee mug to warm them. All night she'd lain in a pool of her own fear, a chill of helplessness engulfing her.

She hadn't been able to save her child. Or those women.

She *had* to help the police find the killer.

"I'm afraid we don't have anyone in custody yet," Devlin cut in. "That's why we're here. We need your help."

Claire nodded. "I'll do whatever I can."

Devlin cleared his throat. "Good. The first victim, Dianne Lyons, was single, twenty-five, blond, a waitress at a local diner in Savannah. She lived with a cat and her boyfriend." He paused. "The second victim, Beverly Bell, was married, thirty-two, a brunette and a professional architect. She lived with her husband and baby."

Claire twisted her hands together. That poor child had been left without a mother. It was all so senseless.

"So far, you and the *Calling Claire* show appear to be the only connection," Devlin supplied. "You didn't know either of the victims, Dr. Kos?"

"No." Claire hugged her arms around her waist, the image of the young women fighting for their lives haunting her.

"You've never treated either of them?"

"No. Did you trace the calls or find any evidence at the scene to identify the killer?"

"Not yet," Devlin said. "We're still waiting on the forensics report. The killer used throwaway cell phones you can pick up at any convenience store. We're trying to pinpoint where the killer purchased them, but it'll take time."

"But you think he'll kill again?"

"Yes." Agent Devlin sigh was filled with weariness. "Do you have any idea why he's calling you?"

Claire shrugged. "The show. It's his twisted way of announcing his crime. He wants the publicity, probably even wants help."

"You do believe the killer is a man?" Agent Devlin asked.

Claire nodded.

"He likes the attention?"

"Yes."

"Do you think you could create a profile?"

Claire nodded. "Yes, but I'll need more information on the murders."

"We can give you access to police files." Devlin paused. "We'll also need to look at your patient files. It's possible the killer knows you personally. He chose you because he wants to watch your reaction."

"Patient files are confidential," Claire said. "I can't let you see them and you know it, Agent Devlin."

Mark stood, his feet clicking across the floor impatiently. "Claire, how can you protect the sick bastard? Don't you understand? He might be gunning for you next."

"First of all, we *don't* know that the killer is one of my patients," Claire said in a guarded voice, unable to admit her own fear that Mark was right, "or that he intends to do anything to me except use me to gain public attention for himself."

"It's too dangerous," Mark said. "Get someone else to cover the show."

"I'm not abandoning the show or running scared." Claire stood, squaring her shoulders and angling herself to face him, although he was pacing so rapidly she couldn't pinpoint his location in the room. "These women, the killer, they're calling me for a reason. I have to find out why, and do what I can to help them."

"I don't want you involved," Mark said.

"I'm already involved."

"But you're too vulnerable," Mark's voice exploded. "For God's sake, in your condition, I don't know why you're even on the radio."

Fury and hurt twisted in Claire's chest. Mark had always been protective, a hero, but at one point he'd respected her work and viewed her as an equal. Now he saw her as a weak, handicapped woman.

"I may be blind, Mark, but I'm not helpless," Claire said, determined to prove she didn't need his protection. And she certainly wouldn't be controlled by a man. "I'm a professional, perfectly capable of performing my job."

"She's right, Steele, she's already involved," Agent Devlin cut in. "We need her. The killer picked her for a reason. She may be the only one who can reach him or figure out his identity."

"Thank you, Agent Devlin."

"But he's right, too," Devlin said. "You are vulnerable, Dr. Kos. We don't know if the killer has targeted you, so we're assigning Agent Steele to work with you."

As some kind of bodyguard?

Claire bristled at the silent implication. How could Mark protect her when he held the power to hurt her most of all?

MARK HALTED, filled with a mixture of anger, fear and disbelief. Didn't Claire realize the severity of the situation?

Using a trained agent as a go-between or bait would be dangerous enough, but a vulnerable blind woman...

It's not just because she's blind.

Damn, the sight of her long, blond curls spilling over her shoulders and those emerald eyes that had once looked at him with passion, and now looked past him, empty and vacant, had totally wrecked his composure.

He'd barely prepared himself to meet her again, yet to see her like this, to know she needed him but refused to acknowledge their past or the chemistry between them...

"You can't be serious." Claire crossed her arms defensively. "I don't need his protection."

"For God's sake, Claire, you can't see. You might not even know if this maniac was following you."

She shivered slightly, and although satisfied he'd made his point, he hated to see her frightened.

"Then why not have a local cop or CIRP provide their own security?" Claire asked.

"You have a problem with my credentials?" Mark's

laser-sharp voice dared her to defy his professionalism and admit his effect on her.

"No," Claire said tightly. "But I am wondering why you left the army."

"My tour of duty was up," Mark answered, unwilling to elaborate on his reasons.

Devlin cleared his throat. "Dr. Kos, you want to help us find this man, don't you?"

Claire's hesitation spoke volumes and gnawed at Mark's pride. Of course she did. The feisty, smart Claire he'd known had not been destroyed by her accident. She simply didn't want to be near him.

Maybe that was a good thing. Maybe it meant that she hadn't totally forgotten him as he'd once believed.

"Of course."

"It's an FBI matter now," Devlin said. "But we will be working in conjunction with the local police and CIRP's security."

Mark watched the sunlight catch the golden rays in her hair, the way she massaged her forehead with her long slender fingers, a gesture he'd seen so many times. He wanted to massage her temple, soothe away her worries, watch her eyes light up with passion the way they once had when he touched her.

"Please review your files, Dr. Kos," Devlin said. "If one of your patients fits the profile of our killer, you have to inform us."

"I'll review them," she said, although she didn't commit any further.

"We also need a list of any men you're involved with," Mark said.

Claire swallowed. "I'm not involved with anyone at the moment."

A sharp pang of relief rifled through Mark, but he ignored it. "Anyone in the last, say, two years. That includes male employees where you work, neighbors, acquaintances—"

"I get the picture." Claire held up a hand. "Do you really think the killer is someone I know?"

"We can't say yet," Agent Devlin said. "We're gathering the same information on the victims. Who knows? We might get lucky and find a connection when we cross-check them." Devlin's coffee cup clattered as he placed it on the saucer. "If you think of anything, Dr. Kos, no matter how trivial, something one of the women said on the phone, something a client told you that strikes a familiar chord or a connection, please inform Agent Steele. He'll be your contact."

Mark shook Devlin's hand, agreed to stay in touch, then watched as he headed to the door. As soon as it closed behind him, Mark turned to Claire. She was facing the fireplace, her back to him, her posture rigid. He wanted to go to her, to hold her and assure her everything would be all right. But a wall had been erected between them, a wall he didn't know how to breach.

And he couldn't relinquish the hurt that had consumed him those first few weeks when he'd gone overseas, thinking she didn't want him.

He had tried to understand. A military life wasn't conducive to family. He should know, having grown up in one. Always moving around. A new city, strange people and faces. Never getting too close because there were always goodbyes. His life belonged to the army. There was no room for anything else.

Now he'd left that behind, and he had to build a new life.

"You should have left, too," she said quietly.

He had once. In fact, he hadn't expected to return from overseas. Another reason he'd decided not to bug her with phone calls when she hadn't shown that day. It had been unfair of him to pressure her for an answer before he shipped out or to ask her to wait for a man who might never return.

And now he had, but he was an empty shell of a man. A man riddled with guilt and the dark shadows of death that only war could bring.

He shut out the thought. Tried to focus on the case. "I don't intend to leave until we catch this guy."

She turned then, that foggy look in her eyes almost too painful to tolerate. "Then I guess I'd better start on that list of possible suspects," she said softly. "The sooner we catch this guy, the sooner you can go."

He ground his teeth, her message loud and clear. She didn't want him back in her life. Just as she hadn't wanted to marry him.

The whisper of her shampoo tortured him as she walked past and claimed the desk chair in front of her computer. His stomach knotted as he realized the changes she'd made to her apartment, her computer, her life. He glanced around the small living area at the bookcase, surprised at its lack of hominess. In Atlanta, Claire's shelves had been filled with books and brass horse sculptures, a collection she'd started with her sister years ago. Claire had loved riding, had often teased that she wanted to take him on a bareback ride in the mountains, or on the beach. He'd always joked that they didn't need a horse to do that.

They had never taken the ride.

Apparently she hadn't brought the sculptured horses with her when she'd moved to Savannah. Had she given up riding because of her visual impairment?

He watched her compile the list and wondered about other changes. She'd once been full of laughter, full of surprises, and grit. The grit was still there, but the laughter had died.

She'd also always been open, honest, giving, loving and passionate. She'd enjoyed sex, had not been shy about the act like other women he'd known.

Had she changed in that respect now, too? Or had she lied about not having another boyfriend?

He clenched his fists by his sides at the mere thought of another man touching her, then reminded himself that he'd lost her long ago. "Why didn't you send me word about the accident, Claire?"

Claire's fingers hesitated over the keyboard and his eyes were drawn to the special program she used. "Because we were no longer a couple, Mark."

The finality of her statement hammered reality home as she turned her back and resumed working at the computer.

CLAIRE FELT Mark's presence behind her as she assembled the list he'd requested, her emotions in a tailspin. How could he show up in her life and demand she walk away from her job? And how could he still have the power to affect her simply with the sound of his voice and his masculine scent?

She had worked so hard to forget him, all the small details that made him special and had endeared him to her heart.

Like the old-fashioned way he opened the door for her, and the way he pressed his hand to the small of her back when he led her into a restaurant. And the way he murmured her name as if it was a lover's caress. The simple hoarse sound of his voice had caused a tingle to spread up her spine.

He wouldn't be murmuring her name in any kind of a lover's caress now.

Especially if he discovered she'd lost their baby.

Besides, time had passed. He probably had another woman in his life. And she was blind, would be a burden to any man, especially one as adventurous as Mark. He liked outdoor sports, parachuting, mountain climbing, skiing, all kinds of activities she couldn't participate in now.

Worse, being close to him only reminded her of the night they'd made their baby.

Forcing the torturous thoughts from her mind, she concentrated on her acquaintances and entered their names into the program, although she felt as if she was betraying them by listing them for the police. But the task had to be done. And it gave her something concrete to focus on besides the fact that Mark was watching her every movement. Even without sight, she felt him following her, gauging her facial expressions, honing in on her fear so he could use it to persuade her to stop hosting her show.

But she'd been on the receiving end of the phone calls, had heard those women's pain-filled pleas, and she intended to help stop the killer. It was the only way she could silence the haunting cries in her mind and atone for her responsibility in the victims' deaths.

Dragging herself back to the keyboard, she plugged in several names. Ian Hall, the new Director of CIRP. Dr. Ferguson, the head of the psychiatry department. Dr. Kurt Lassiter, another psychiatrist. She paused, remembering the lunch they'd shared the week before, they way he'd touched her hand when she'd reached for her water glass. She'd sensed he wanted more than lunch, but she hadn't encouraged a relationship.

Shaking off the uncomfortable feeling that he'd been angry with her when she'd declined his invitation to a movie, she added a few other names: Billy Mack, a counselor on staff, and two of the orderlies who helped with the patients, Ray Foote and Ted Cleaver. But she couldn't possibly remember the entire staff at CIRP. The police would have to check the hospital personnel records.

Next, she added Drew Myers, the producer of the radio show, and his assistant, Bailey Cummings, but Bailey was no more than a college intern. And Drew had been nothing but a friend. Then there was Arden Holland, the janitor. Deciding he was too old to fit the profile and not agile enough to pull off a murder and escape, she dismissed him completely.

Remembering Agent Devlin's request for her pa-

Chapter Three

Mark accepted the list from Claire. Working with her was going to be hard, watching her struggle to maintain her independence with a handicap even worse.

But not touching her would be the hardest thing he'd ever done in his life.

He had wanted her the first moment he'd seen her.

Ironically, they had met in a Starbucks when he'd been on leave for the weekend. Her hair had brushed his shoulder as she'd turned to grab a packet of sweetener. When she'd laughed and said that she was a coffee addict, he'd looked into her gorgeous eyes, and they'd immediately connected. A week later, he'd taken her to dinner. A day later to bed. The romance had been fast, sometimes sweet, but very seductive. And the sex had been mind-boggling.

But the breakup—inevitable.

He was, after all, his father's son, and didn't know how to hold on to a woman.

But at least his father had been a hero in the military. Had received a distinguished award for bravery tient records, she mentally ticked down the list, wondering if any one of them could have orchestrated the killings. Joel Sanger, a young man in his late twenties, had experienced a psychotic break after a plane crash. Recently he had exhibited violent tendencies toward women. She also had to consider her newest patient, Richard Wheaton, a man she suspected might be suffering from DID, dissociative identity disorder. Richard had been traumatized as a child. Now his behavior was erratic. She'd only begun to scratch the surface of his problems.

Could one of them be responsible for the deaths?

If so, and she started asking questions, would he try to kill her next?

and heroism in a recon mission. Had died in the line of duty serving his country, rescuing prisoners of war a few years ago.

Mark saw the faces of his fallen men in his mind's eye. Even though the army had hinted at giving him a commendation, he had refused it. He didn't deserve to be rewarded when his friends lay six feet under, their families still mourning.

"There are other employees." Claire broke into his thoughts, indicating the printout of names she'd given him, "but you'll have to obtain those from CIRP."

"I'm sure Devlin is on it." His gaze dropped from her rose petal mouth to the paper, and he skimmed the list, his fists tightening. "I'd like to interview the people on this list as soon as possible."

Claire ran a finger over her watch, obviously reading the braille settings. "Most everyone will be gone by now."

He nodded, then realized Claire couldn't see him. She'd never look into his eyes with that same sweet lust again. He had to clear his throat to talk. "They leave at five?"

"Not always, but by eight or nine, everyone's pretty much cleared out except for the janitorial staff and security guards."

"Then I'll start tomorrow." He folded the paper and tucked it inside his jacket pocket. "What are your plans tonight?"

A frown creased her brow as if she was surprised he asked. "I'm going to the studio for the show."

"You can't be serious?"

Her chin rose a notch. "Of course I'm serious. I told you I wouldn't give up my job."

"But a woman was murdered last night, Claire. You must be shaken by her phone call and that creep's message to you."

"That's exactly the reason I have to go." She picked up the phone. "If the killer wants to connect with me, I have to be there when he calls."

"Is that what the legal advisors of the show suggest?"

She hesitated. "They're concerned, but it's important to present the image that I'm cooperating in trying to find this madman. We're going to set up a separate line, too, so we can transfer the calls and the public won't have to listen."

"The research center is using you for free publicity." He moved so swiftly and grabbed her arm that she startled and dropped the phone. "Don't do it, Claire." His gaze latched on the curve of her cheek, her slightly parted lips, a tiny scar at the corner of her chin that hadn't been there before. He couldn't stand to see her hurt again. And he wanted to reach out and touch that scar. Kiss away the pain that had caused it. "Please, Claire, stay home."

Her breath whistled between them, soft, yet full of tension. Once it had vibrated with want, desire, heat. Now he felt only anger.

"I can't, Mark. Besides, the station is tightening security for me. Now, if you intend to work on this case, either help me or leave and request another agent." She reached for his hand, firmly lifted his fingers away from her arm. He caught her fingers in his for the briefest of seconds, savoring her touch, feeling her warmth seep into the cold places he'd lived with since he'd lost her a year ago.

A tense second passed between them, fraught with old memories, and need. He was just about to reach out and brush an errant hair from her cheek when Claire swallowed. "Let me go, Mark, so I can phone the station to send over a car."

He dropped her fingers, aching at the loss and reminding himself that he couldn't get personally entangled with Claire again. His men had died and he'd walked away alive, at least physically. Mentally he was a mess. He didn't deserve Claire. He wasn't sure there was even enough of him left to give her what she needed either.

Still, he refused to leave her unprotected. "Forget the car. If you're going to the radio station, I'll drive you."

"No—"

"The subject is not up for debate, Claire. I'll let the station security know." He smiled, his next words half threat, half promise. "Since I've been assigned to protect you, I intend to stick to you like glue."

At one time she would have welcomed that. But this time, her lip trembled, and she had no reply. She gathered her purse, then he slid his hand to the small of her back to guide her to the door. Instead of leaning into him, warming to his touch as she once had, she pulled away, reached for her cane and walked ahead alone, her chin held high. The cane clicked ominously on the floor in front of him, its sound mimicking a soldier's march.

His heart twisted in response—her dismissal was a firm reminder that everything between them had changed.

GRATEFUL FOR the glass window separating her and Mark, Claire kept her head down, her focus on preparing for the evening show. The car ride had been excruciating, the close quarters too confining for comfort.

She had wanted to touch Mark so badly it hurt.

Memories of her accident assaulted her, playing havoc on nerves already destroyed by the mere feel of Mark's hand pressed possessively against her back. Riding in his old Thunderbird convertible again with the wind tossing his scent toward her had only reminded her that once she'd been happy, in love.

Before he had left. Before she'd lost their child.

An image of a dark-haired little baby froze in her mind. She imagined the soft weight of its body, the little hands reaching for her, the sound of its cry.

The radio signal buzzed, jerking her from the image. Claire exhaled to compose herself, then checked her watch, indicating to Drew that she was ready to start.

Keep it strictly business.

Unfortunately, Mark had joined Drew, rattling her newfound philosophy. She didn't have to see to know that his dark gaze was trained on her, or to remember its effect. His big muscular body could be intimidating, his military persona heightened by his air of authority.

In bed, that commanding attitude had excited her because underneath that tough facade, he was a pussycat.

The buzzer sounded again, and she winced, ordering herself to focus on the show.

"You're tuned in to WKIA, and this is *Calling Claire*, with Dr. Claire Kos." She hesitated. "I'm saddened to report that another woman was murdered in Savannah last night. Her name was Beverly Bell. According to police reports, she was strangled. It's also possible her death was connected to the murder of Dianne Lyons. If you have information on either woman, or their murders, please call the Savannah police." She recited the phone number that had been established by the police for incoming calls, then lowered her voice.

"Sometimes it's difficult to move on after a tragic event in your life, whether that tragedy is a divorce, the loss of a loved one or a breakup. If you'd like to talk, or share tips on how you've overcome a loss, please call me at 555-3456. We'd love to hear from you."

The first caller was experiencing the empty-nest syndrome. Claire suggested the woman get a job or join a volunteer organization or club, something to add a new purpose to her years. "Use this stage of your life to focus on yourself and your mate, rediscover all the reasons you fell in love, rekindle the romance, travel, enjoy the activities you haven't been able to do with children underfoot."

The buzzer dinged, and she accepted the next few calls, a series of young women in their twenties searching for Mr. Right. They discussed the common pitfalls women fell into by looking for men in bars, then she helped each of them make goals for the future, honing in on ways to judge if a man was a commitment phobic.

Next, a young woman who'd lost her husband in a

car accident phoned, her trembling voice clutching at Claire's heartstrings. "He was only thirty," Sonya said. "He had just gotten a promotion, we'd bought a house, wanted a baby…"

"It's tough to be the one left behind," Claire said sympathetically. "You have a void in your life, and you're grieving, but you also feel angry, as if he deserted you."

"How did you know?"

"Because I've experienced those feelings, Sonya. My father died when I was young. I remember the anger, and the sadness. And of course, the questions— why him? Why me?"

"He was so young," the girl murmured in a strained voice. "It's not fair."

"No, it's not fair, but anger is an honest, natural emotion, a stage of the grieving process," Claire said. "You have to deal with it so you can move on."

"That's just it…I don't know if I can."

Claire tensed and checked her watch. Nearly midnight. The same time she'd received the other two desperate calls. Would the killer call again tonight and take another life?

"Yes, you can, Sonya. Talk to your family, your friends, tell them how you feel, vent your anger, your fears, your grief, so you can heal."

"I'll try. There's something else…there's this guy…"

"Someone who's interested in you?"

A sniffle passed over the line. "Yes, but I feel so…guilty."

"Experiencing survivor guilt is not uncommon,"

Claire said slowly, not trusting her own emotions. "You don't believe you're entitled to enjoy life again, to even laugh or have friends. Or take on another lover."

"That's exactly how I feel," the girl said, her voice trembling.

"But you deserve happiness," Claire said softly. "Your husband loved you, right?"

"Yes."

"Then he'd want you to enjoy your life just as you'd want him to do if you had died."

Claire wondered if she'd ever be able to take her own advice.

MARK SAT, transfixed by Claire's words. Did she know what had happened to him overseas?

No, she couldn't…

He saw his best friend's face as he lay wide-eyed in the dirt, Abe's dirt-coated hand gripping Mark's as he inhaled his last breath. And in his mind, he saw Abe's wife, her face ashen with grief, the burning accusations in her eyes. Why had he survived when her husband had been taken?

Mark pinched the bridge of his nose, grateful Claire couldn't see his expression. No doubt his emotions were plainly written on his face.

Instinctively, he knew Claire was right. Abe wouldn't want him to stop living or to blame himself for his death. But rational thoughts couldn't absolve his guilt.

"Tuck those memories of your husband into a special place in your heart," Claire said. "And keep them safe. But keeping those memories doesn't mean you can't make room for more."

Mark studied Claire through the glass window. Was that what Claire had done? She'd put their memories into another place so she could make room for someone else?

It shouldn't matter to him. In fact, he should be happy for her. Claire deserved the best.

What did he have to offer her anyway?

"That's all the calls we have time for tonight," Claire said, jazz music floating into the background, "but join us again Friday night. This is Dr. Claire Kos wishing you a safe night and a happy tomorrow."

Mark stood, and watched as she organized herself and walked to the door. He was amazed at how well she maneuvered her surroundings with her cane. She must have counted the steps, memorized the layout. He admired her spunk and her ability to adapt.

But she was so vulnerable, a perfect target. What would happen if she was on a crowded street or in a strange building? What if someone followed her?

She would be virtually helpless, not knowing if they were even there....

"Great job, Claire," Drew said as she approached. "The show went smoothly tonight."

Claire sighed. "Thank goodness. When I realized it was midnight, I couldn't help but worry."

Drew began cleaning up the sound area, filing CDs. "Maybe your bad luck is over."

Mark eyed him, knowing everyone in contact with Claire had to be treated with suspicion. According to his notes, this show had been Myers's creative doing, so he most likely had a vested interest, either money- or careerwise, in making it a success.

Would Myers do something drastic to spike ratings? Something like murder?

"Thanks for letting me sit in." He shook Myers's hand.

"I take it you'll be back?" Myers asked.

"Yes."

"That's really not necessary," Claire said.

He glared at her, then remembered she couldn't see him. She must have sensed his reaction though, because she shook her head, an impatient gesture he'd seen so many times when she'd been frustrated.

"I'll see you Friday, Drew."

Drew said good-night, and Claire headed for the front of the station. Mark trailed behind her, allowing her the small victory by letting her lead. She would not win the war, though, and get rid of him.

Not until this killer was caught.

She halted at the front door and reached for her cell phone.

"Put it away, Claire, I'm driving you home."

"That's—"

"I know, not necessary." He sighed. "Listen, Claire, it's obvious you don't want me around, but we've agreed this killer has to be stopped, so the sooner we start working together, the sooner we can accomplish that."

She snapped her phone shut.

"Every moment doesn't have to be a battle."

"Then stop treating me like I'm an invalid."

He couldn't help it. Claire brought out all his protective instincts. And more.

"You're being overly sensitive," he said, aware his comment would irritate her. "And I don't think of you as an invalid, but you have to cut me some slack. I'm just doing my job." And trying to be considerate. *Something you once would have admired.*

She flinched as if he'd hit her, and he felt about two feet tall. "Fine, let's go to the car."

He glanced outside and noticed it had started raining. "Wait here, and I'll bring it around."

"I can go with you."

"Don't be silly. It's pouring down rain, Claire."

"I can hear the rain, Mark. I'm not stupid."

"No, just stubborn." His temper had reached its limits. He and Claire had never bickered over trivial things, had simply fallen into step together as if they'd been dancing all their life. Now, they were totally out of sync. "I'll be back in a second."

She folded her arms. "Pull up directly in the center, and I'll meet you outside."

He gritted his teeth, then jogged outside to the car. Her independence was a good thing, he reminded himself.

Unless it made her do something stupid, like put herself in the hands of the killer.

CLAIRE TOSSED and turned through a fitful sleep. When she'd first arrived home after her accident, she'd argued with her sister about moving to Savannah. Paulette wanted Claire to stay in Atlanta so she could take care of her. As if Claire really wanted to be indebted to her sister.

Once again, she dreamt that she'd been locked in the house with Paulette, forced to endure her condescending attitude and feel like an invalid, a burden to feed her sister's martyr attitude.

That nightmare had drifted into one of her accident. The bloodred water had sucked her under. She'd struggled and fought, the iciness gripping her until she'd finally floated into a surreal state, blinded by a sharp light. Then someone had pulled her from its clutches, dragged her to the surface and tossed her ashore, as if she should go on. But she hadn't wanted to go on.

Save yourself, Claire.

But she couldn't…

Mark suddenly appeared, battling enemy soldiers and being shot, then falling to his death. She saw the blood, so much blood, but there was no red, only black. Her scream boomeranged her back to the hospital where she'd awakened with a throbbing emptiness swelling inside her. She was all alone. So alone.

Another cry escaped her and she jerked awake, only to finally fall fitfully back to sleep and dream of the women callers, begging for help, their final cries ringing in her ears.

Then the killer was after her.

She was running blindly through the marsh, wondering if it really mattered if she lived or died…. So much had happened. She'd lost so much already.

She jerked upright, trembling and breathing hard,

then froze, reminding herself her nightmares had held only partial truths. She reached for the picture frame and traced her fingers over the heart-shaped opening where her baby's picture should have been. It was empty. Her baby was gone.

But Mark was still alive.

The woodsy scent he'd left behind wafted around her, and she gripped the tangled sheets with fisted hands.

Oh, Mark was very much alive.

Alive and strong and so damn masculine she wanted to scream every time she got near him. Scream for him to hold her, to take away the pain, to make love to her and magically change everything back to the way it used to be.

Dreaming of what could have been was futile.

Throwing off the covers, she swung her legs over the side of the bed and listened to the familiar early morning sounds that represented comfort and safety. The lull of the ocean outside. An occasional seagull soaring overhead. The whisper of the wind against the wooden frame.

This was her life now. Claire Kos—psychologist. Workaholic. Radio personality.

Loner.

Checking her clock, she realized she had only half an hour before Mark would arrive. Last night, they'd made plans to go to the police precinct and review the files on the victims before she met with her first patient. She headed to the shower, but she stumbled and nearly fell, barely catching herself on the rocking chair she normally kept in the corner.

It wasn't in the corner anymore, but stood in the center of the bathroom doorway.

Someone had moved it.

Claire's breath caught in her chest, a sick feeling sweeping over her. Then a strange odor assaulted her— a medicinal scent. Someone had been inside her cottage. Was he still there?

HE WANTED CLAIRE.

He'd wanted her for so long. Even with her eyes glassy-looking with pain, she was still the most beautiful woman he'd ever met. Beautiful and strong and gutsy and...alone.

Just like Dianne Lyons and Beverly Bell.

Who did they think they were shunning him?

Claire had, too. Even though he had saved her once...

Yes, he had, and he could forgive her for turning away. If she'd only listen now. If only she'd come to him.

He watched her curtains flutter in the wind and wondered if she'd awakened. Did she know he'd slipped inside her cottage to watch her sleep? That he had almost reached out and soothed away her cries, had nearly touched that silky hair, had almost brushed his lips across hers when she'd tossed the covers in her nightmares.

He knew all about nightmares.

Just as he knew Claire's hidden desires. Her need for comfort in spite of her fierce independent nature.

Her need for a strong man.

And he was strong. In spite of his injuries, the past few days he had proven he was still fit.

He brought one of her scarves to his mouth, closed his eyes and inhaled her scent, then imagined his lips tasting hers, imagined taking off his clothes, having her healing touch slide across his skin. With her, he would be whole again. And he would make her whole, too.

He would make her forget Mark Steele.

Claire would see it that way one day, too.

Until then, he'd have to be content to watch her from afar. And he'd take what he could from the others, proving his strength as his hands tightened around their slender throats, drawing the life from them....

Chapter Four

Mark hadn't slept all night for thinking about Claire. He scrubbed a hand over his bleary eyes, parked in front of Claire's cottage and climbed from his Thunderbird. Early morning sunlight fought for existence through the hazy sky. Mark could relate. Ever since he'd been carried from that prison camp and honorably discharged from the military, he felt as if he'd been slogging through a dark fog searching for his way.

Searching for a reason to live.

Claire.

Keeping her safe gave him purpose. But it was all tangled up with this new job and the past. Only she wanted nothing to do with him.

Perspiration dotted his forehead as he approached her front door. For just a moment, he allowed himself to move back in time. He had come to pick her up for their second date. He'd worn his uniform. She'd opened the door, her hair blowing in the breeze, her lips parted in invitation, her eyes lit with anticipation.

Tonight, those eyes wouldn't be able to see him.

He braced himself for the disappointment, along with the war that raged within him over not touching her.

Finally, shaking off his own selfish need, he punched the doorbell. A second later, Claire appeared.

"Who is it?"

"It's me, Mark."

When she swung the door open, she was still wearing a white linen nightshirt that caught in the morning breeze and fluttered around her thighs. Sunlight shone through the sheer fabric, giving him a glimpse of her sleek body, of golden skin, narrow hips, a flat stomach, then lower to the heat that had once sated his desires.

God help him, but he wanted to push up that gown and sink himself inside her now.

"Mark…I'm not dressed."

"Obviously. Do you always answer the door like that?"

She jerked her head up, defensive. "No."

He was just about to lecture her on the fact that a killer was stalking Savannah when he noticed she was shaking. Her face was pale, too. "What's wrong?"

"I…I think someone was in my cottage."

He gripped the doorjamb, instincts alert. "When?"

"Now," she whispered, "or…maybe last night."

He instinctively drew her against him, using his body as a shield between her and the inside of the cabin. "Are they still inside?"

She shook her head. "I don't know."

Fury iced his veins. Of course she didn't. "Stay here. I'll check it out."

"No, let me go with you."

She clutched his arm, and for the first time since he'd seen her again, she held onto him. He hated that fear had brought them to this point. "All right, Claire, but stay behind me. And if I say run, you damn well better do it."

She clung to the back of his shirt as he drew his weapon and moved inside, her body pressed against him. The living room was dark, as was the rest of the cottage. Claire didn't need lights, a bitter reminder of her condition.

He scanned the kitchen, then moved to the bedroom, his throat working when he saw the tousled covers and imagined Claire stretched out on the pale yellow sheets. Had someone been inside, watching her sleep?

The room was empty, though. So was her tiny bathroom.

Finally, he lowered his gun and turned to her. She stumbled into him, then pushed away to regain her balance. "Why didn't you call for help?"

"I was going to, but then you showed up."

He paused, calming himself, reverting back to professional mode. "Why do you think someone was inside?"

She took a calming breath and squared her shoulders as if she realized she'd shown a weakness. "The chair in my bedroom was moved from the corner."

He frowned.

"Someone had to have moved it," she clarified as if she'd seen his expression. "It's important that I keep everything in its place."

He knew it cost her to admit that.

"And in my bathroom…" she said in a low voice. "My perfume, cosmetics, they were all moved around, left open on the counter."

"Anything else?"

She nodded and hugged her arms around herself. "Some scarves were missing from my drawers."

Mark gritted his teeth. The other women had been strangled with scarves. Had the intruder taken Claire's as a memento or did he plan to use them to choke his next victim?

"And…" her voice broke. "I found a rose."

Dammit. The killer had also left a crushed rose in each victim's hand.

His stomach churned as he spotted the flower on Claire's pillow. Was it some kind of calling card to let her know she would be his next victim?

A FEW MINUTES LATER, Detective Black arrived to process the crime scene, although he'd told Claire he doubted they'd find any fingerprints. She belted a robe around herself and made coffee, then clasped the cup to her while the men combed her cottage.

"You didn't hear anyone last night or this morning?" Black asked.

Claire shook her head. "No. I…I don't know how I missed hearing him. I'm a light sleeper."

Mark grunted in disapproval. "I don't like this."

"Neither do I," Detective Black said. "As soon as we're finished, I want you two at the station to review the case."

Claire agreed, grateful when they allowed her to

spray the air with freshener to absorb the pungent medicinal odor. Finally she took a shower. Taking refuge beneath the spray of hot water was heavenly, a place to gather her control, away from the all-knowing eyes of her former lover. She hated being vulnerable, hated having to admit she was unaware that someone had been in her bedroom while she was asleep.

The thought sent a chill through her that no amount of hot water could dissolve. She'd thought her other senses would compensate for her lack of sight.

Composing herself, she toweled off and dressed in a denim skirt and cotton blouse. Thankfully, the therapist at the rehab center had tagged her clothes, so she didn't worry about looking mismatched. She blew her hair dry and twisted it into a clip, then added a hint of powder and mascara. Makeup was more difficult, but she'd practiced. A touch of lipstick came next. Heaven help her, but her hands were so shaky she almost missed her mouth.

Seconds later, she was seated in Mark's car, the silence stretching between them as jarring as the juts in the road that led to Savannah.

"I really wish you'd leave town for a while," Mark said as they entered the police station.

Now that the shock was wearing off, anger plucked at Claire. "I don't intend to be victimized," she said in a firm voice. "And when this man entered my house and moved my things around, that's what he did."

"Claire…"

Mark's husky tone reeked of concern, tugging at feelings she didn't want to revisit. "I'm not going to argue over this, Mark. Now, let's look at those police reports. I want to know exactly what we're dealing with."

A sigh followed, his only reply.

Things turned even more awkward when they arrived at the station. She hated looking so helpless, having to take Mark's arm as they climbed the steps.

Hated even more wanting not to release him.

Detective Black ushered them into a room, then spread the police reports of the two victims on the table. Mark began to study them, leaving her completely out of the loop and magnifying the fact that she was a burden now, not his equal.

"Read me the contents of the reports," Claire said.

"You don't need to know the details," Mark said, that protective air vibrating around him.

Claire sighed. "How can I create a profile of the killer if I don't know the facts?"

Mark hesitated, his reluctance obvious.

"You'll have to be my eyes, Mark," she said, frustrated that she needed him. "Now read me the report."

He shuffled the papers, then read in a monotone. "The first victim, Dianne Lyons, was single, twenty-five, blond. She lived with her boyfriend and cat and worked as a waitress at a local diner in Savannah. She was found lying facedown in the sand at Serpent's Cove, strangled and blindfolded with a scarf. Forensics is still analyzing the scarf."

"What about the autopsy report?"

Mark exhaled in a rush. "Claire—"

"I need to know everything, Mark. I'm not going to fall apart."

The papers rattled again. "Death by strangulation. No other injuries, no apparent signs of struggle, no foreign DNA found, including scrapings from under her fingernails."

"So, she didn't fight her attacker?"

"If she did, the M.E. didn't find evidence. But she was injected with enough Percoset to make her sluggish, probably so she couldn't fight."

"That's interesting. Some killers get off on watching their victims struggle." Claire paused. "And Percoset? I wonder why the killer chose that particular drug and where he obtained it. Maybe he works in some kind of medical job, or perhaps he was injured and got hooked on pain killers while in treatment."

"Or maybe he's a junkie." Mark drummed his fingers on the table. "I'll make sure we follow up on all those theories."

"She wasn't raped or sexually assaulted?"

"No."

"Hmm. Do the police have any suspects?"

"Boyfriend's alibi stands up. He was with another woman at the time." Mark's foot tapped on the floor. "They're still questioning friends, relatives, acquaintances."

"What about the second woman?" Claire asked. A surge of emotions crowded her throat at the thought of the poor motherless baby left behind.

"M.O. is the same. She was found facedown, blindfolded and strangled. Again no signs of struggle, no DNA found, no sign of sexual assault."

"Suspects?"

"Husband claims he was in a business meeting in Charleston. His story checks out."

"How about her co-workers?"

"Nothing so far, but they're still being questioned."

"And the women didn't know each other, or run in the same circles?" Claire asked.

` "No mutual friends or acquaintances that the police have discovered. Dianne rented a small apartment in the low-rent part of town, Beverly and her husband own a home in the historic district. Dianne ran with the working class, Beverly with the society crowd. No mutual clubs, volunteer organizations, hell, they didn't even shop at the same clothing or grocery stores."

"Odd." Claire considered the information. "Usually a serial killer typecasts his victims to resemble the person he lost or his abuser."

"I know." Mark shifted. "Your show seems to be the only common factor so far."

Claire bit her lip, the idea that she might have attracted the killer and led him to these women too daunting to fathom. No, the show hadn't drawn him to kill; it was the other way around. He was using the show to flaunt the murders and gain publicity. "There has to be a connection. We just haven't found it yet. Keep looking." She paused. "Are there photos?"

Mark's foot began tapping again, a sign of distress. "Yes."

"Is there anything distinctive about the way the women are lying? Are they posed?"

He shuffled the photos, obviously spreading them across the table. "Both victims were lying facedown.

Clothes were wrinkled and dirty, but again, no signs of sexual abuse."

"Are their arms behind them, above their heads?"

Mark sighed. "Stretched above their heads."

"Hmm, they're lying facedown, as if they're ashamed of themselves, even in death."

Mark stilled beside her. She could feel the tension in his body. And as much as she detested doing it, in order to understand the killer, she had to get inside his head. Try to think like he would.

"He calls them bad girls," Mark said. "But these women aren't prostitutes."

"Still, they're not perfect in his eyes." Claire shifted. "The fact that there's no sexual abuse is interesting. It suggests he may be impotent or disabled in some way. And the way the hands are stretched above them, it shows his sense of control and power, and their lack of it. He wants them to be submissive. He gets off on proving how strong he is."

Mark's tapping became faster as he continued examining the photos. "Dammit."

Claire's hands tightened in her lap. "What is it?"

"The rose. It's red just like the one on your pillow this morning, except this one is dead, crushed, the petals scattered around her body in the sand."

Claire inhaled sharply. So it *was* the killer who had been in her cottage. Why had he left her a live rose when he'd left his victims holding a dead one?

MARK FISTED his hands around the steering wheel in a white-knuckled grip. The killer had definitely been in

Claire's bedroom watching her sleep this morning, touching her things, dropping a flower on her pillow as if marking her as his next victim. He'd known it, but seeing the photographs of the women in death had still sent a shock of reality through him. For a moment, Claire's face had replaced those of the victims.

He'd damn near lost it.

Grappling for control, he reminded himself that the killer hadn't warned any of the other victims. Maybe he didn't plan to murder Claire, maybe he was just using her....

He wished to hell he could believe it.

Tires squealed as he took the turn. Claire's hands were clenched around the seat belt, her sightless eyes wide and staring into space. Guilt forced him to slow the car; he was scaring her. "I'm sorry."

"It's going to be all right, Mark."

He tossed out a sardonic chuckle. "How can you be so calm?"

"You're frantic enough for both of us."

He laughed again, but his laughter held no humor. Claire had always been calm in the face of a storm, the reason she was such a good psychologist, where he'd let his temper rule his actions.

Except on the battlefield. He had to rein in his emotions to do his job, and he had done it. The controlled soldier, meticulous with details, focused on the hunt when tracking down a war criminal, religious about tamping his personal feelings.

Except for the night he'd lost his men. Then he'd fallen apart.

But he had to maintain his control now.

Because Claire was involved. This battle was personal. She was in danger.

"You can drop me off at the center," Claire said quietly.

"Not a chance, Claire. I'm going in to start questioning the staff."

"Oh…right."

He neared the Coastal Island Research Park's main facility, and slowed, frowning at the cluster of people gathered around the front steps. "Is the center hosting some special event today?"

"No, why?"

"There's a crowd out front." He parked and cut off the engine, scanning the group. "Dammit. The press is here, too." He opened the car door, furious. Claire stepped out with her cane, and he halted. "Wait here, Claire, let me see what's going on."

"This is my business environment, Mark. I'm going with you."

He scrubbed his hand over his chin and met her in front of the car, then grabbed her hand and placed it on his arm. "Then hold on."

She tensed, but finally acquiesced, and he led them through the throng until they were close enough to hear the speaker. He recognized Ian Hall, the Director of CIRP, from the photos Devlin had shown him. Cameras were trained on him, while he held a microphone in his hand.

"Ladies and gentlemen, I appreciate your time today," Hall said. "On behalf of CIRP, I want to publicly express our concern over the two young women who phoned Dr. Claire Kos. She's a valuable member of our team, and has done an outstanding job combining her practice and lecturing on various topics, the very reason she was chosen to host the radio talk show. CIRP is doing everything in our power to help the police investigate these violent deaths."

"Although the police haven't verified they're dealing with a serial killer," a lanky reporter said, "all evidence suggests that fact."

"I heard they're calling him the Midnight Murderer," another reporter said.

More reporters jumped in, shouting questions at once.

"Is Dr. Kos available to speak to us?"

"Yes, where is she?"

"Does Dr. Kos know the identity of the Midnight Murderer?"

Mark shoved Claire behind him. "I can't believe this. He's milking the crimes to get publicity for CIRP."

"I can assure you," Hall continued, "Dr. Kos is doing everything possible to assist the police. I will arrange an interview for her when we speak again."

"Like hell you will," Mark muttered.

A tall reporter in front of him turned and noticed Claire's cane. Seconds before she pounced, her eyes turned hawkish. "Dr. Kos is here now! Let's hear what she has to say."

The other reporters elbowed their way toward them like vultures. Mark encircled Claire with his arm and pushed through the crowd. "Dr. Kos has no comment."

"Mark—"

"Come on, Claire, you're not going public."

He dragged her up the stairs, fending off hands and microphones, then shot Ian Hall a threatening look. "Get inside, Hall, we have to talk."

Hall gaped, but recovered enough to paste on a smile for the camera. "That's all for today, but thank you for coming. We'll keep you posted."

One of the reporters grabbed Mark's arm. "Sir, are you a policeman? FBI?"

"He's Mark Steele," another reporter shouted. "He's the guy who survived that explosion overseas."

Mark gripped Claire harder. Dammit, he hadn't thought about being recognized.

"Lt. Steele, can you tell us what happened to your men?"

Mark gritted his teeth and pushed the horde of reporters away.

"Mark?" Claire angled her head to him in question.

He had refused all interviews so far. He didn't intend to talk now and open his wounds to the public.

"Get inside, Claire," he barked.

Hall ducked inside behind Mark as the crowd moved forward. Mark shut the door, then yelled at a security guard to bar anyone from entering.

Ignoring the reporters' references to himself and pleas to talk to Claire, he turned to Hall. "What the hell are you trying to do, get Claire killed?"

Chapter Five

Claire had never heard Mark lose his temper before. Although he'd probably taken lives while in the army, she hadn't sensed that he was a violent man.

But this Mark was someone she didn't know.

What had happened to him this past year to change him? What had happened to his men?

Stories of posttraumatic stress syndrome rushed to her mind. She wished she could see his face, look into his eyes and study the shadows, ask him about the demons that had followed him home. But she and Mark no longer shared that closeness.

"I don't know who are you, Mister, but I suggest you back off." Ian Hall's voice held a hint of fear he'd tried to disguise with his command, but Claire recognized the emotion.

"Special Agent Mark Steele, FBI," Mark said. "I'm working with Dr. Kos to find the Midnight Murderer."

"I see. Well, welcome to CIRP, Agent Steele," Hall said, changing his tone. "As I said in my press announcement, I'll do everything possible to aid your investigation."

"Then you don't mind answering a few questions?"

"Of course not."

"And you won't interfere when I interview your employees?"

A hesitant second followed. "My staff will assist you in every way they can, but you will, of course, have to go through our security channels."

"Meaning?"

"Meaning certain areas and files are restricted." Claire heard the rustle of Ian's starched shirt as he straightened his tie, a nervous movement she'd noticed before. "But I will make certain you have access to any pertinent information."

"Then you won't be holding any more press conferences and offering Claire up as the proverbial cure for your bad publicity."

"Mark," Claire said sharply, infuriated he'd speak to her boss about her.

"He has no right, Claire," Mark said.

"That's between Dr. Hall and myself," Claire argued.

"No," Mark said in a cold voice. "Not anymore. I'm in charge of this case. You'll both follow my orders."

Claire balked. She'd discuss his tone with him later, away from her co-worker. "I have to go to my office," she said. "I have patients scheduled."

Mark's hand went to the small of her back. So natural, yet so unnatural now that things had changed. "I'll walk you, then I'd like to talk to some of the staff members on your list, Claire."

She pulled away slightly, just to make a point. Mark might be in charge of the case, but he wouldn't control her. "Let's go." The sooner he questioned her fellow employees and friends, the sooner they'd solve this case, and he'd be gone from her life.

Then she wouldn't be reminded of how much she wanted him, or be tempted to worry about the darkness tainting his voice, or the fact that she desperately wanted to reach out and hold him.

And she'd never have to reveal her secret.

WHILE IAN HALL showed Mark the main building of the research park and coughed up a general sales pitch and description of the other buildings, Mark memorized the layout, the various types of research projects taking place and the names of the heads of each department. He also kept an ear and eye on Hall, searching for any hint that the man might be involved in the murders.

It was a little far-fetched that the new director would actually murder to gain attention, especially considering the prior scandal associated with the center. On the other hand, what better way to promote goodwill and garner publicity than by swooping in to save the entire city from a crazed killer? The mystique of Nighthawk Island certainly had attracted some odd characters. For all he knew, Hall could have hired or brainwashed someone into committing the crimes.

As they made their way back to Hall's office, the director turned to him. "Where do you plan to start, Agent Steele?"

"Since Claire…Dr. Kos, seems to be the only link between the victims, I'll need to question everyone— her colleagues, business acquaintances, friends."

"Then let's head to the psychiatric department." Hall gestured toward the door. "We can take this corridor through the breezeway that connects the buildings."

A few minutes later, Hall introduced Mark to Dr. George Ferguson, the head of the psychiatric department, then excused himself for a conference call. Ferguson was probably in his midthirties, had dark hair, and was all business. Although there were two male doctors in their sixties on staff, Claire had dismissed them already, saying they didn't fit the profile because of age and in the latter case, agility.

"I'm sure you understand why I'm here," Mark said, seating himself in the chair across from Ferguson's desk.

"Yes, we've all been concerned about Claire since the phone calls."

Mark stiffened. "How well do you know Dr. Kos?"

Ferguson frowned. "We're co-workers and friends. We've consulted on a few cases."

"You hired her?"

"Yes."

"Did you know either of the women who were murdered?"

"No."

Mark sighed. "What's your theory on the killer's reason for phoning Claire?"

"It's that damn show," Ferguson said. "I've never been in favor of TV and radio pop psychology shows.

Dispensing advice without a complete assessment of a patient is dangerous. The entire setup opens the door for liability cases. Malpractice insurance has skyrocketed in the past few years already."

So, he was just as concerned about money as the people's welfare. "Dr. Kos was aware of potential problems?"

"Yes, she took precautions, but I'm still not in favor of using the show as a venue to make Ian Hall look good."

"You don't get along with the new director?"

"We're amicable. I simply disagree with a few of his tactics." Ferguson fiddled with a paper clip. "Our jobs and the work we do here is invaluable. We don't need to advertise it."

"Your specialty is psychotic disorders?"

"Yes, but I treat a variety of illnesses, as does Claire and most of the doctors here. Since Claire's lecture tour, we consider her our resident specialist on families in crisis."

Mark took note of the man's desk; his office was immaculate, neat, orderly. Even the pushpins in the bulletin board behind him were in a straight, even row. "Do you think his calls to Claire seem personal, that he knows her?"

Ferguson drew a repetition of small circles with the clip as he spoke. "I believe he chose her because she's in the public eye. Serial killers want to be noticed. They're often from abused homes, are insecure and seek out attention."

"That's pretty much what Claire said."

Ferguson smiled, revealing perfect teeth. "We normally agree."

Mark clenched his jaw. "Are you single?"

Ferguson twitched. "Yes."

"Ever been married?"

"No, no time for it." Ferguson shifted, jiggling a paper clip into his palm. "What does my marital status have to do with this case?"

Mark shrugged. "Nothing, maybe. But I have to ask."

Ferguson's eyebrows shot up. "I get it. You think someone who knows Claire is the killer, and you're looking at me as a suspect?" The doctor leaned back, barked out a laugh. "That's absolutely ridiculous."

Mark simply stared at him. "It's routine. I'm questioning all of Claire's business and personal acquaintances. Then we can eliminate people and determine the real killer's identity."

"All right, then allow me to clarify the situation, Steele. I don't need to kill women or make clandestine calls to Claire to get attention. I might be single, but it's not for lack of interest by the female population."

Ahh, the doctor was arrogant and cocky, too.

"So, you've dated Claire?"

"Not exactly."

"What does that mean?"

Ferguson's fists tightened. "That's none of your business."

Mark leaned forward, arms crossed. "Let me guess, you asked her out, but she turned you down?"

Anger darkened Ferguson's eyes. "I'm not the only

one she refused. Claire hasn't been very social since she came on board. I wanted to change that."

Mark just bet he did. "Who else approached her?" When he didn't respond, Mark pressed him, "Look, I'm going to find out sooner or later, so you might as well tell me. Help me narrow down the suspect list, it's the only way to catch the real killer."

Ferguson shoved his blunt nails through his hair. "Half the male staff wants to date Claire, Steele. Our newbie, Kurt Lassiter got turned down just last week." Ferguson dropped the clips on the desk, scraped back his chair and stood. "Now, I believe we're finished."

"One last question. Where were you the past two Friday nights at midnight?"

"At home in my office, preparing notes on a case."

"Can anyone verify that?"

Ferguson's eye twitched slightly. "No, I was alone." He gestured toward the door with a flick of his thumb. "This meeting is over."

Mark thanked him. He didn't trust Ian Hall or George Ferguson. But he obviously had a few more names on the list to sort through.

He wouldn't stop until he questioned every staff member. Kurt Lassiter was next.

And if one of them intended to get revenge on Claire because she'd rebuffed him, Mark would make sure he put a stop to their plans.

CLAIRE REVIEWED her patient files again, the same two names popping up as suspicious. Joel Sanger and Richard Wheaton. But she refused to turn them over to the cops for questioning, not unless she was certain one of them was the Midnight Murderer.

She had scheduled appointments with both men for that afternoon, hoping to determine their moods and check their mental stability. She breezed through two other consultations first; one, a woman with an eating disorder, the second, an alcoholic father who had been forced into treatment during a custody battle. Both faced a lengthy recovery process.

When Joel Sanger strode in, she immediately sensed an air of angry tension surrounding him. From his file, she knew he was in his early twenties, with wiry brown hair. A tattoo of a lizard snaked up his left arm and a nose ring dangled from his nose. Loud rap music pounded from his CD player, the lyrics full of violence toward women.

She tried not to read too much into his choice of music, but his behavior proved he had little respect for females. He did, however, enjoy racy sex. In their last session, he'd used some colorful language and invited her to participate.

"Hello, Joel."

"Yo." The music blared on.

"Can you turn that down, please, so we can talk."

"What if I don't feel like talking?"

Claire grappled for a nonjudgmental, even tone. Reacting to a patient would only work against her. She had to maintain an air of authority to be effective. "Then I tell your parole officer that you aren't cooperating."

He released a string of expletives, and she reached for the phone.

"Dammit, lady, don't call."

"The music?"

It faded into silence.

"Thank you." She gestured toward the sofa. "Would you like to sit down?"

"No."

During their first two sessions, she'd felt his animosity, but the last two visits, he'd been more talkative. He appeared to have regressed.

"What's on your mind today, Joel?"

He broke into a bitching session about his ex-wife. "She oughta get a job as a prison warden."

"I thought you didn't want her to work," Claire said, remembering their earlier discussion. Joel had some archaic views about women; he thought their place was in the home and their function to serve men. His wife had finally balked when he'd turned violent one night, and she'd pressed charges. But she'd dropped them under the stipulation that he receive counseling.

"Hell, I don't, I'm just saying she's mean as a pit bull."

"So, you two aren't getting along?"

He paced across the room, fiddled with the blinds. They screeched as he repeatedly opened and closed them. "We're okay now. She made up for being bad."

Claire's skin crawled, the caller's words echoing in her ears. *She's been a bad girl, Claire. A very bad girl.*

"What do you mean, she made up for being bad?"

A sardonic chuckle escaped him. "In bed." He shuffled toward her, his voice growing menacingly low. "Just like all bad girls, Doc, she had to be punished."

His breath, foul from cigarette smoke, brushed her face as he invaded her space. "She took it real good, though, Doc. Took her punishment like a lady."

Claire's heart pounded, but she refused to show her fear or he would win. "Did you hurt her again, Joel?"

His eerie laughter wafted around her. "Hell, Doc, she damn near died from pleasure."

ON THE WAY to meet Lassiter, Mark phoned Devlin. "Just checking in to see if you've got anything new."

Devlin cleared his throat. "No. We tried to track down where the killer bought the roses, but it's impossible. Street vendors sell them by the dozens."

"Any of our suspects have a flower garden? Work for a florist or a gardening service?"

"We're looking into that now."

"Good. What about the cell phones?"

"They're sold in blocks to convenience stores and retailers. We've traced both to local stores, but neither of the clerks remember who purchased them. We can check credit cards, but cash is harder. Any luck on that end?" Devlin asked.

"Nothing specific. I'm just beginning to question the staff here. Ian Hall professed to be cooperating although he was holding a press conference when I arrived. He wanted to make sure he received public accolades for his assistance in the investigation."

"He won't be so cooperative if we confiscate restricted files on personnel."

"True. How about the other family members and acquaintances of the victims?"

"Dianne Lyon's boyfriend checks out although there's a strange guy in her apartment complex we're looking at. He has a record for assault."

Mark exhaled. Would they be lucky to find the guy so soon? For Claire's sake, he hoped so. He didn't want her in jeopardy.

Of course, when the case ended, he'd have no reason to stick around….

"The second victim's husband lawyered up," Devlin said. "We don't have enough evidence to hold him. We're running a nationwide check on recently released prisoners and mental patients, especially ones with violent tendencies or criminal records. Maybe something will turn up there."

"I'll keep digging on this end," Mark said. Devlin agreed to stay in touch and Mark hung up just as he reached Lassiter's office.

A redhead sat at the receptionist's desk entering data into a computer. "Excuse me, I'd like to see Dr. Lassiter."

She pivoted and glanced up at him over tiny square glasses. "He's not here at the moment. Can I make you an appointment?"

"Just tell me where to find him."

"May I have your name, sir, and what this is in reference to?"

Mark flashed his ID. "FBI, ma'am, official business."

Her eyes widened, a flustered look crossing her face. "Oh, goodness. Well, let's see, he just rushed off to Dr. Kos's office for a minute. She had a problem with one of her patients."

Mark thanked her and hurried down the hall, praying Claire wasn't in trouble.

CLAIRE FELT FOOLISH for phoning Kurt Lassiter, and immediately wished she hadn't. In fact, her first instinct had been to call Mark, but she'd choked it back, knowing he would ask questions that she couldn't answer if she wished to maintain her professional integrity.

Or maybe she'd been afraid she'd leap into his arms and succumb to temptation and kiss him.

She'd probably read way too much into Joel Sanger's comments anyway. If a psychologist searched for something devious in a patient's rantings, ninety percent of the time he would find it, even if it were simple mad rantings. Besides, her patients had to trust that they could divulge those innermost thoughts without judgment or retribution.

"I'm sorry, Kurt," she said. "I overreacted."

"Claire, if you're worried about a patient, you were right to call me. In fact, you can call me anytime, day or night."

"I know, and thanks." She rubbed her hands up and down her arms to warm herself. "I suppose those awful phone calls to my show and those women's murders are making me jumpy."

"They should have you spooked," Kurt said. "If you want me to take over as Sanger's doctor, I will. Just say the word."

"No, I want to continue."

"But if he's dangerous or involved in these recent murders—"

"I'll let you know if I discover anything specific that points to him as the killer."

Kurt moved up behind her, and she tensed. Twice, he'd asked her out, and she'd turned him down. She didn't fully understand her own reasons.

He had been nothing but a gentleman. A friend and a professional she admired.

Yet he wanted more.

But since her accident, she'd shut herself off from personal relationships, especially with men, hiding away behind her visual impairment and pain as if she'd closed the curtain on her life. Besides, something about Kurt...bothered her.

He hesitated behind her, and she sensed his desire, then his hands fell over hers, and he squeezed her fingers. His hands were softer than Mark's, not as callused or as strong. But they were gentle. "Claire, I'll do whatever I can for you, here at the office, or...wherever."

Claire closed her eyes, gave into the moment and leaned against him, willing herself to feel something for him, to be able to accept his comfort. Unfortunately, the only face that filtered through the darkness was Mark's. The only arms she wanted around her were his, too.

"Claire?"

Mark's dark voice boomed behind her. She pulled away from Kurt, feeling as if she'd somehow betrayed Mark. But that was ridiculous.

Mark didn't still care for her, did he?

Chapter Six

Seeing another man touch Claire sparked Mark's jealousy, but he reminded himself that their relationship had ended a year ago. Still, emotions moved inside him—a deep sense of loss mingled with a hunger to have her back again.

His instincts kicking in, Mark sized up the man beside Claire. He was around five-eleven, lean with sandy blondish hair, and intelligent eyes. Not as confident or arrogant-looking as Ferguson, but he supposed women might find him attractive. Still, something about the beadiness of his eyes triggered Mark's suspicions.

Was Claire really interested in him?

Do your job. If you get emotionally involved, you might not be able to protect her.

"I'm looking for Dr. Lassiter," Mark said.

Claire pulled herself away, and the man gave him a damning look as if he had interrupted an important moment.

"This is Dr. Lassiter," Claire said. "Kurt, this is Lieutenant, I mean Agent Steele. He's with the FBI."

Kurt? Claire had said she wasn't involved with anyone, but she'd used this man's first name, implying their relationship was on friendly terms. Obviously not as personal as Lassiter wanted though....

"Ahh, you must be working on the serial killer case." Lassiter strode forward and extended his hand.

"Yes, I am." Mark shook his hand, finding the other man's grip lacking. And it didn't take a rocket scientist to see that Lassiter had his sights set on Claire.

Would he kill to get her attention? Or would he threaten her to make her pay for refusing his overtures?

Mark dropped his hand and faced Claire. "Did something happen, Claire?"

Claire moved back to her desk. A safety net, Mark realized. The desk provided a barrier between her and both men, put them all back on professional ground. He didn't like being delegated to the same category as Lassiter.

"We were just discussing a case," Claire said.

A case? *Right.* "You were worried about a patient being dangerous?" He cut his gaze toward Lassiter, then back to Claire, gauging their reactions. "Do you think this patient has something to do with the phone calls you received at the show and the women's murders?"

"I can't divulge patient information and you know it, Mark."

Of course, she could discuss it with Lassiter. "But we agreed—"

"You told me if I thought a patient should be treated as a suspect to let you know." She thumbed a strand of hair back into place. She'd twisted her curls into some kind of knot at the base of her neck, which looked conservative yet sexy as hell and revealed the creamy skin of her throat. And those little spirally wisps that dangled around her cheeks made him itch to reach out and touch them.

Mark dragged his mind from her throat and the tempting thought of kissing it. "And?"

"And I will, but I can't do that unless I have more reason. Even if I thought a patient might be dangerous, it doesn't mean he's the killer you're looking for."

She had a point, but he didn't like it. "Maybe not, but if you find someone you suspect, Claire, I expect your cooperation."

She jutted up her chin. "Yes, well, if that's all, I have another patient to see."

"Fine," Mark said. "I need to ask Dr. Lassiter some questions." He turned to the doctor. "Why don't we go to your office."

Lassiter gave him a wary look, but gestured toward the door. Just before he exited himself, Lassiter suggested to Claire that they have dinner.

Mark frowned and vowed to make certain Claire had other plans.

CLAIRE HAD NO IDEA why she'd let the sound of Mark's voice draw her away from Kurt.

Or did she?

You still have feelings for him.

No, she couldn't. But it wasn't fair to lead Kurt on, either.

Maybe in time she could see Kurt as more than a friend, but now…now there was too much turmoil in her life. Now, she had to focus on finding this killer before he hurt anyone else.

What if one of her patients turned out to be the killer?

All the more reason to resume work and forget the edge that had tinged Mark's voice when he'd walked in. His brusqueness probably had nothing to do with finding her nearly in Kurt's arms. He was simply uptight about the case.

After all, he hadn't even called to check on her when she hadn't arrived at the airport or later when she'd returned the ring. He'd walked away and never looked back.

Maybe his proposal had been a desperate attempt to connect with someone before he shipped out and he'd regretted it later; she'd heard of similar instances with other service men.

Latching onto that rationale, she turned back to work.

She made a few notes in Joel Sanger's file, then prepared for her next patient, Richard Wheaton, the man she suspected was suffering from DID, dissociative identity disorder, a condition once referred to as multiple personality disorder. Although she'd read case studies on victims with the disorder, Wheaton was the first case she'd witnessed personally.

So far, during her sessions with Wheaton, she'd glimpsed two alternate personalities—a young child and a bitter, troubled adolescent. Neither resembled the withdrawn young man she'd first encountered.

"Hello, Richard."

"Claire." His low-pitched mumble was so quiet that she could barely hear him.

She wished she could observe his body gestures, too, it might give her insight into his other personalities. With his permission, she videotaped her sessions, and Dr. Ferguson had reviewed them with her, describing Wheaton's physical gestures. He'd also agreed with her speculations.

Wheaton hadn't responded well to male doctors so they both agreed it imperative she remain as his primary therapist, at least in the beginning stages.

"How are you today?" Claire asked.

He held back near the doorway, tentative as usual when he first arrived. "All right," he said in that barely audible voice.

"Come in and sit down, Richard. I'm glad you're here."

He didn't reply, but shuffled in, taking short jerky steps, then settled into a seat. She pictured him perched on the edge of the sofa as Ferguson had described, running his hands self-consciously through his short wavy brown hair. According to Ferguson, Richard seemed awkward, his nose and ears too large for his elongated face, his appearance having made him the butt of ridicule by his peers as a child.

Those tauntings had been the beginning of his problems, or at least the ones she'd detected. She suspected childhood trauma, maybe abuse had caused more severe damage.

"Richard, today I thought we'd explore your childhood and family. Tell me about your parents."

She heard his feet click on the floor and realized he'd started rocking himself back and forth. He always resorted to the comforting behavior when she broached the subject of his family. "Your father died when you were five?"

"Yes," he said in a small, screechy voice.

"Do you know what caused his death?"

"An accident," he whispered.

"What kind of accident?"

"He…he got hit by a car."

Claire nodded in encouragement. "The accident happened on the street where you lived?"

His feet clicked up and down. She sensed the tension in the air, heard his breathing become more labored. "In…front of my house."

"And you saw the accident?"

"Y…es." He careened, a low-pitched childlike sound. "St—stop it, Mommy. Stop it. Don't hit Daddy."

The careening intensified. His voice became juvenile, like that of a five-year-old.

"Richard, where is your mommy?"

A muffled sob escaped him, and he dragged in ragged gulps of air. "In…the car."

She was certain he had never revealed that information to anyone, not even the police. "Is your mother driving the car?"

His feet rocked back and forth wildly as he began to cry. "Yes. Mommy, stop it. You're hurting Daddy."

Claire rose and moved toward him, then sat down beside him to calm him. "Take a deep breath, now, and tell me what you see."

He sniffled. "Daddy..." he cried, "Daddy on the driveway, all bloody. Don't die, Daddy. Regina needs you."

"Who's Regina?"

"My sister."

Claire paused. "Where's your mother now, Richie?"

"Mommy...she's coming at me. She...she's mad, she jumped out of the car, she's screaming, she's going to get me. No!"

He suddenly flung his arm up and knocked Claire to the floor. The back of her head hit the coffee table. She clutched the edge for support, her jaw stinging.

He bolted off the couch and strode to the window in thunderous steps, his voice loud and booming. "Hush, stop crying now. I took care of her. She can't hurt us anymore."

Claire rubbed the back of her head and stood, slightly dizzy and more cautious now. This voice wasn't the whinelike cry Richard had spoken in earlier. It was a deep, threatening masculine voice filled with rage.

"How did you take care of her?" Claire asked softly.

"That bitch," he bellowed. "I made sure she's gone and she's never coming back!"

According to the police report, Richard's father had been killed when he was five. His mother had died when he was thirteen. Supposedly Richard had witnessed both his parents' deaths.

There hadn't been any mention of a little girl.

The report hadn't suggested that he was responsible for killing his mother. But was he?

And had there been a sister or was she another one

of Richard's personalities? And if the sister had been real, what had happened to her?

Fear seeped through Claire.

Richard's abuse and trauma explained his personality disorder. But he also fit the profile of the Midnight Murderer.

MARK'S CONVERSATION with Lassiter didn't go much better than the one with Ferguson. He refused to give up information on Claire's cases or his relationship with Claire. And when Mark questioned him about CIRP and the possibility of illegal or unethical experiments, he'd grown almost hostile, defending the center's reputation and his co-workers' ethics.

Mark had finally threatened to haul him in for questioning, reminding him that his refusal to answer questions made him look guilty. Finally he gleaned a tidbit of information—Lassiter had been engaged three years ago, but the woman had supposedly cheated on him, and he'd canceled the wedding.

He sensed bitterness, but was it enough for Lassiter to turn against all women?

Mark would push Claire to see how much she knew about the man, then check out Lassiter's past. Maybe an interview with the ex-fiancée would offer more on his character, determine if Lassiter had ever been violent.

He checked his watch and hurried down the corridor toward Claire's office. He intended to take her to dinner before her radio show. But first he stopped to question the nurses in the psychiatric department. He introduced himself and explained his reasons for being there. Eileen Putter was the head nurse, in her late fifties with graying hair and an obvious propensity for food. Wynona seemed the opposite, a thirty-something, no-nonsense rail-thin woman with a permanent frown.

"What can you tell me about the doctors on staff?" Mark asked.

"What do you mean?" Wynona said.

"Has anyone acted suspicious lately? Could one of them have a grudge against Dr. Kos or women in general?"

"Are you kidding?" Eileen said with a laugh. "Most of the doctors think they're God's greatest gift on earth. Especially Dr. Ferguson."

Which might make it hard for him to accept rejection.

"What about Dr. Lassiter?"

Wynona frowned. "He's always been very professional. But I did hear that his ex-girlfriend died suspiciously."

Mark's pulse jumped into overtime as he removed a small notepad and began to jot down notes. "How do you mean suspicious?"

"Heard she committed suicide," Eileen said.

"But they never found a note," Wynona added.

"How did Lassiter react?"

"He seemed upset," Eileen said. "I felt sorry for him at the time. First she dumped him, then she ups and kills herself." She hesitated, her eyes going wide. "You don't think…no, it couldn't be."

"We shouldn't be talking about Dr. Lassiter," Wynona said, as if they suddenly realized they'd forgotten loyalties. "He really is a good doctor."

"Have any of his patients had problems with him? Any complaints?"

The two women traded questioning looks, but clamped their mouths shut.

"Like I said, we shouldn't be gossiping," Wynona said.

Eileen latched on to the other nurse's arm. "That's right, we could lose our jobs."

"Two women have been murdered," Mark said. "Other lives may be at stake."

They glanced nervously around, then Eileen leaned closer. "Well, there was a female patient who complained. She said he…he came onto her."

Mark frowned. "Did anyone corroborate her story?"

"No, as a matter of fact Dr. Kos questioned the girl, but she didn't believe her."

"But you do?"

Eileen shrugged and Wynona bit her lip. "The girl did have some questionable bruises on her arms. She claimed he grabbed her, but he denied everything. According to him, she got volatile, and he had to restrain her."

Lassiter's name moved up a notch in Mark's mental database of suspects. As if they regretted the confidence they'd shared, the women rushed off, so he headed toward Claire's office.

When he arrived, she was locking up for the night. "Claire?"

She jerked her head up and anger knotted his stomach at the sight of a fresh bruise on her cheek. He lifted his hand, brushed his fingers across the red welt, his breath tight in his chest. "Who did this?"

She blinked and dropped her head forward as if to shield the wound from him, but he cupped her chin in his hand and refused to let her hide. "Who hit you, Claire?"

"One of my patients got upset. It's nothing, Mark."

"The hell it's not. A patient attacked you and you call it nothing?"

"He simply reacted to a traumatic memory, and I happened to be in the way. Accidents go with the territory." She pulled away, but he caught her arm, refusing to let her run. His heart was pounding.

"His name, Claire?"

She hesitated, then shook her head. "I can't tell you that, Mark."

"You can't or you won't?"

"Both. If I don't protect my patients' privacy, they won't confide in me. Then I'm useless."

"Dammit, Claire, you told Lassiter? And how helpful will you be to your patients if you end up dead?"

She sighed, anger tightening her mouth. Or was it fear? "Kurt is another psychologist, Mark. I was asking his professional opinion."

"That's not how it looked to me."

She chewed on her bottom lip. "My relationship with Kurt is none of your business."

He wrapped his hands around her arms, determined to make her realize she might be in danger. He didn't want her to fall for Lassiter's innocent boy act.

"You can't trust anyone, Claire, not right now. It's too dangerous."

This time she raised her chin. Even though she couldn't see him, he felt her eyes bore into his as if she could. "I know how dangerous trusting a man can be, Mark. After all, I once trusted you."

Her words cut him like a knife. But regardless of her feelings toward him, he had to protect her.

"Did you know that Lassiter's ex-fiancée died suspiciously?"

The quiver of her bottom lip indicated she hadn't.

"And one of his patients made allegations against him."

"She was manic," Claire said. "And those claims were never substantiated."

"It does make you wonder, though," Mark said. Claire suddenly seemed apprehensive, as if he'd started the wheels of doubt turning in her mind.

Good. It was better she be paranoid and alive than trusting and dead.

CLAIRE STRUGGLED to calm her tumultuous emotions on the ride back from the station. She didn't want to distrust her patients, her friends or her co-workers. At CIRP, she had started to finally feel safe. To heal.

But the killings, and Mark's warning, had shattered that sense of safety.

She struggled to remember the details of Kurt's fiancée's death and his female patient's complaint. His fiancée had had emotional problems, had been anorexic but trying to recover. Then she'd become obsessed with

Kurt. A suicide hadn't been expected, but in retrospect, Kurt had professed that there might have been signs. Signs she'd kept well hidden. He'd blamed himself...or so it had seemed.

His patient had been young, suffering from a manic-depressive disorder. Her bouts of hysteria had been occurring daily and had gradually grown more acute. Then that day, she had claimed Kurt had hinted at trading sexual favors for drugs.

Claire had listened to her story, but she hadn't believed her. It was easy and not uncommon for patients, especially female patients, to blame their doctors, to accuse their male caretakers of sexual harassment. The girl had a history of not taking responsibility for her own actions. Of lying to get attention. She'd been angry and going through withdrawal from her cocaine addiction.

Had Claire been wrong in not listening to her more carefully? Had she been so blinded by Kurt's kindness to her that she'd been oblivious to the truth?

No...

"You still like Italian food, don't you?" Mark asked as he parked at Antonio's, a place they had frequented when they'd dated.

Mark's voice broke through the haze of her troubled thoughts. They had shared a love for rich spicy food just as they had coffee and making love in the mornings.

"Claire?"

"Yes, I still like Italian food."

"Good." He opened the door, and she inhaled to calm herself. This was a business dinner. Not a romantic night with her lover.

He led her to the back of the room, the delicious scents of marinara sauce and garlic bread wafting around her. Without asking, he ordered the half and half combination pizza they'd shared when they'd dated.

"Wine, Claire?"

Yes, she would love some to ease the tension. "No, thanks, I have to concentrate on the show tonight."

"You wouldn't if you'd give it up until this case is over."

She fumbled with her water glass, silently willing herself not to make a fool of herself in front of Mark. He hadn't come for romance. "Don't start again, okay?"

"I…I'm sorry, Claire, but I'm worried about you."

And don't pretend you care. "I'll be fine. After all, the FBI and the Savannah police are both working on the investigation." She toyed with the napkin in her lap. "Why are you really working with the FBI, Mark? I thought you intended to make a career out of the military?"

His hesitation resonated with tension, reminding her of the reporter's comment. "I received a medical discharge," he said in a gruff voice.

Claire's hands tightened around the napkin. Were his injuries visible? She wanted to reach out and touch him, make sure his face hadn't changed, that he hadn't been hurt. But she'd given up that right when she'd returned his ring. "What happened?"

"My men and I were ambushed. I took some shrapnel to my shoulder."

"But you're all right?" She hadn't detected a limp or a cane. And he wasn't in a wheelchair.

"I'm fine, although it affected my marksman abilities," he said in a dark voice.

"And the other men with you?"

He hesitated. "They weren't so lucky."

"They didn't survive?"

His breath rasped out. "No, my entire unit was lost."

Claire's heart squeezed at the anguish in his voice. She couldn't help herself, she reached out and placed her hand over his. The brief contact sent heat curling in her belly, resurrected hidden desires and yearnings that she had only felt with Mark. His hands were so strong, callused, wide, his fingers long and blunt. But they had been so magical. "I'm sorry, Mark. I'm sure you did everything you could to save them."

His hand stiffened beneath hers while his silence suggested he blamed himself. "Do you want to talk about it?"

"No."

The waitress appeared to deliver their food and Mark pulled away, his dismissal of the subject evident when he began to talk about the pizza. She allowed him to give her a slice, then she concentrated on eating, afraid she'd dribble food on her clothing and not even know it. He lapsed into silence, their conversation during the meal stilted.

Back in the car, she tried to pull herself together and stop worrying about Mark. He didn't want her concern, and he obviously didn't intend to share his problems.

But his presence in her life, along with his comments about Kurt Lassiter, added to her mounting distress. She detested living under this constant level of distrust.

And she sensed that Mark's attitude toward Kurt held a personal edge to it that had nothing to do with Kurt being a suspect. Mark had sounded almost jealous.

No, Mark was not jealous. Why would he be? He hadn't written or called when he'd received the ring.

The army had been his life. He'd told her that when he'd decided to leave, he'd chosen it over her.

But she was still surprised he'd accepted the discharge. He could have stayed on, taken a desk job.

But Mark was not a desk job kind of man.

Had his friends' deaths affected him so deeply that he would give up his career goals? Was he battling inner demons? Or had she read too much into the threads of darkness she heard in his voice?

"We're here."

Claire gathered her cane and purse. "Thanks for the ride."

He sighed. "I'll park the car and meet you inside in a minute."

"You don't have to baby-sit me during the show, Mark."

"I want to be there if there's another call."

Claire relented and nodded, then climbed the steps to the station and opened the door.

"Evening, Ms. Claire."

It was Arden, the janitor who was always so nice. "Are you done for the night?"

"Yes, ma'am," he said. "Got to go home and see about the wife. She's not feeling too well."

"Tell her hello for me, and I hope she's better soon."

He held the door for her, then left, and she entered the radio station. Inside, she headed straight to the elevator, but when she reached it, her cane hit a sign on the floor.

"It's out of order," a man said in a low voice. "We're working on it now, Miss. You'll have to take the stairs." He cleared his throat. "Do you need help?"

"No, thank you." Claire frowned, an uneasy feeling gnawing at her. But she shook it off. Mark had definitely stirred her paranoia with his comments, but she refused to give into it.

After all, the man was just a repairman. And if the elevator was broken, there would be other people in the stairwell.

Sweeping the cane in front of her, she turned and walked toward the door that led to it. A dank odor assaulted her when she entered. Cigarette smoke. Maybe sweat. A chill washed over her. The stairway had always been drafty, she remembered, pausing as she heard footsteps behind her. Hating her visual impairment for adding to her paranoia, she hesitated, then climbed one level. The footsteps remained the same distance behind her.

She stopped, deciding that it might be another crew member. Maybe even Drew. But the footsteps halted as well.

"Hello, who's there?"

An eerie silence echoed through the cement walls. "Drew?"

Again, no one answered. And there was that odd odor.

She gripped the stair rail and took another step, hoping she'd imagined it. But it lingered—some kind of medicinal scent similar to the one in her cottage the day she'd had the intruder.

Her stomach clenched in response, and she called out again, "Who's there?"

But this time the whisper of a voice drifted toward her, "Bad girls must die, Claire. But you're not a bad girl, are you?"

Claire gripped the stair railing and ran, stumbling up the stairs. Panicked, she misjudged the distance between steps and lost her footing. Her knees hit the concrete, she bit back a cry, and tasted blood.

Then the whisper of the man's breath brushed her cheek, his singsongy voice piercing the air around her.

Chapter Seven

"Where's Claire?"

The station manager glanced up at Mark over an assortment of CDs as he readied for Claire's show. "She hasn't come in yet."

"What?" Alarm rang in Mark's mind. "I dropped her off in front a few minutes ago."

Drew shrugged. "Maybe she went to the ladies' room."

Mark breathed in and out. "Right." So, why did he suddenly feel so uncomfortable, as if his sixth sense was alerting him to danger, just as it had seconds before the attack on his men?

He checked the clock. After he'd parked the car, he'd phoned Detective Black at the Savannah P.D. for an update before he'd entered the building. That had been a good ten minutes.

His gaze scanned the room. Through the glass window, he noticed a rose on Claire's desk. It wasn't in a vase, but wrapped in dark green tissue. The warning bells clanged louder. "Where did that come from?"

Drew followed his gaze, his expression perplexed.

Then he spotted the rose and frowned. "I don't know. It wasn't there when I arrived."

"Did you leave the area?"

"I forgot some notes and ran back to my office. I couldn't have been gone more than a few minutes."

Mark dashed inside the room and checked the card. The envelope was plain white, no florist's logo. And it was addressed to Claire.

His anxiety level rose another notch. He slid the card from the envelope.

Dear Claire,
Rose are red, violets are blue, a single red rose means I love you.
Your secret admirer

Damn. If the killer had dropped it off personally, that meant he had been in the building.

He might still be around. And Claire was nowhere to be seen.

His heart pounding, he called security to check the building, then rushed from the room, and scanned the hallways but saw nothing. He raced to the ladies' room and knocked, then poked his head in. "Claire?"

It was empty.

He ran toward the elevator, fighting full-fledged panic. The bell dinged, it opened, and a brunette exited. "Excuse me, have you seen Dr. Kos?"

"Who?"

He stifled a curse. "Dr. Kos? The psychologist, she hosts the radio show, *Calling Claire?*"

"Oh, yes, she was in the lobby a few minutes ago."

"Was she with anyone?"

"No. She went into the stairwell."

Why would Claire take the stairs? It didn't make sense.

He thanked the woman, then spotted a security guard and explained the situation. "Make sure all the exits are barred. Stop anyone who enters or tries to leave."

Then he vaulted toward the stairs at a sprint. Just as he opened the door, Claire stumbled out, grasping for the wall, her cane bobbing between them. Her hair was disheveled, her face flushed, her breathing rapid. A swift inventory revealed bloody knees and a scrape to her arm.

He grabbed her to pull her to him, but she pushed at him. "Let me go!"

"Claire," he said in a ragged whisper, "it's okay, it's me."

"What?"

"It's me, Mark." He gently shook her. "You're safe now."

She bit down on her lip, emotions clouding her face. His stomach clenched. His own primal need overcame reason, and he dragged her into his arms, pressing her head into the crook of his shoulder. Someone had obviously been after her, but she'd survived. Thank God.

Unable to stop himself, he stroked her back, dropped a soft comforting kiss into her silky hair, then closed his eyes and held her.

FOR A BRIEF FEW SECONDS, Claire savored being in Mark's arms, her earlier ordeal having shaken her to the core. Mark was real. Strong. Safe.

Or was he safe?

No, he had hurt her…

Still, she was trembling so badly she couldn't bear to pull away. His familiar scent washed over her in a comforting caress, although his chest heaved up and down erratically as if he'd been on the run as well.

"Claire, thank God you're all right."

She nodded against his chest, her trembling subsiding slightly. But she was still afraid to speak, afraid her voice would reveal the terror rippling through her.

He brushed her neck with his fingertips, then lifted her chin toward him. She felt him scrutinizing her face, searching for injuries, and she desperately wished she could see his expression, that the darkness that had clouded her vision for the past year would lift and allow her to look into his eyes, just one more time. Then she might be able to read his emotions, understand the feelings that had drawn him away from her, and the truth that had brought him back into her life.

But she couldn't allow herself to fall back into the trap of wanting him, needing him. She was much too vulnerable. Besides, why would he want a life with her now that she was imperfect?

She didn't want pity, or for him to feel responsible or guilty. She would never be a burden to anyone. She'd told her sister the same thing and she'd meant it.

"What happened, Claire? Why were you in the stairwell?"

She licked her lips. "The elevator was out, so—"

"The elevator isn't out, Claire."

As if to punctuate his statement, the familiar elevator chime sounded. A shiver rippled through her. Mark must have felt it because he rubbed his hands up and down the sides of her arms.

"But there was a sign, and a man…in the lobby. He told me they were repairing it."

"The elevator was fine when I came in. And I didn't see a repairman."

Claire swallowed. "He…I don't understand." Or did she? The man who'd been in the stairwell, he'd been posing as a repairman to trap her. And she'd been so gullible.

Mark's silence reverberated with the same realization.

"He must have followed me into the stairwell," she finally whispered. "I heard footsteps behind me and called out, then I stumbled, and he was there."

Mark's fingers tightened around her arms. His breath brushed her cheek. "What did he do then? Did he hurt you?"

Claire's mind raced back. "He bent over me, then whispered that warning about bad girls." Or had she been so terrified she'd imagined the breathy whisper of the man's voice, imagined him talking about bad girls? It had seemed so real, yet one minute he'd been there, the next minute he had disappeared like a ghost in the wind.

"God, Claire." Mark released a string of expletives. "He was in your recording room. He left you another rose."

Claire's legs nearly buckled. So she hadn't imagined the man, the voice. "But we were alone, Mark…he didn't hurt me."

"Not this time," Mark said gruffly, "but don't you see, Claire? He's toying with us, with you. He'll be back, and next time...well, next time, we have no idea what he'll do."

Claire dropped her head forward to shut out the images bombarding her. Images of the other two women lying facedown in the sand. Strangled. Alone.

Dead.

Was the killer taunting her to find him, or would she become one of his victims?

THE NEXT FEW MINUTES were chaotic. Mark had wasted valuable time holding Claire, yet the only way he could convince himself she was safe was to feel her in his arms. Breathing. Warm. Alive.

Switching back to professional mode, he ushered her into the station, ordered Drew to get a first aid kit, then hustled to talk to security. But as he feared, the killer had already escaped. He'd either come in disguise or he'd been so nondescript no one had noticed him.

Mark spent the next half hour reviewing the tapes from the security cameras, studying each and every person who had entered and exited the building.

No one stuck out, in fact the traffic had been minimal. The guard had watched the tapes with him and had identified every person on them. How had the man gotten in without being seen?

Unless he was someone who worked at the station...

"I want a list of every male employee in the building, along with a list of any visitors, repairmen, workmen, couriers, etc. who've entered the building today," Mark said.

The security guard nodded. "It'll take some time, but I'll get it to you."

He phoned Detective Black. "Listen, Black, Claire was attacked tonight in the stairwell. And the killer left her a rose."

"Damn. He's getting ballsy."

Too much for comfort. "I don't know if his visit to Claire means he's going to kill again tonight, but you might want to stake out the beaches."

Black agreed. "That's a lot of territory, but I'll get some extra men on it right away."

"Good, we need to catch this SOB before he strikes again." He clenched his fists, silently finishing the sentence.

Before he comes for Claire.

CLAIRE GRAPPLED for control while she described her ordeal to Drew.

"Dammit, Claire, I don't want you going anywhere in the building alone."

She smiled, his display of anger unusual. Mark was another story. He'd been like a boiling pot ready to explode.

"I'm fine, Drew. Besides, if the man had wanted to hurt me, he could have."

Drew applied antiseptic to her knee, then placed a bandage on her scrapes. The smell reminded her of the odor she'd sensed in the stairwell, and in her house, yet it wasn't quite the same. What was that scent? Some kind of surgical soap maybe? An antibiotic cream?

"You're damn right he could have," Drew said. "I'm tightening security. You won't be alone anywhere in this building, not even for a minute."

"Thanks, I appreciate your concern." She started to stand, but he caught her hand.

"Claire, did Agent Steele tell you about the rose?"

She swallowed hard. "Yes. You didn't see who delivered it?"

"No, I wish I had."

Claire squeezed his hand in return. "It's not your fault, Drew. Besides, we aren't certain the rose is from the killer."

He hesitated. "You're right, I suppose. The card says it's from your secret admirer."

Claire stiffened. "I don't have a secret admirer."

"Ahh, Claire," Drew said in an uncharacteristically thick voice. "That's not true. You're a beautiful woman. A lot of men are interested in you."

For the first time since she'd met Drew, she detected a hint of personal interest. Heat radiated from his hand to hers, the tension palpable. "Thanks for saying that, Drew. But I'm a mess right now. It's a good thing this is radio, not television."

"It wouldn't matter, you'd look great anyway."

Claire blushed and pulled away. "Well, thanks again. Now, let's get ready for the show, and pray we don't receive another strange call tonight."

MARK WATCHED Claire and Drew, his gut tightening when Drew squeezed Claire's hand. The first time he'd met Drew, he hadn't considered the guy a serious suspect. He was medium height, stocky build, wore glasses. Exactly the type of person to blend in, not attract attention.

And he could certainly go anywhere in the building without raising suspicion.

Drew had supposedly been in his office when the rose arrived, but he had had access to the programming room—what if he had placed the flower inside before everyone arrived? His concern when Mark had called for him to get first aid had seemed genuine, but Mark had heard of criminals hurting their victims, then showing up at the scene to rescue them and act as their savior.

Jotting down a reminder to check out the man's past, he moved into the room and cleared his throat.

"Mark?" Claire asked.

"Yes."

"Did you find anything?"

"I'm afraid not." He glanced at Drew for a reaction, but Drew was watching Claire as if he couldn't take his eyes off of her.

Was he reading too much into Drew's friendly concern or could the man be the secret admirer who'd sent the rose? The Midnight Murderer?

But how could he help with the show and phone in at the same time?

It was impossible.

Unless the message had been prerecorded…he'd check out that angle.

"Listen, Claire," Drew said. "I have some business I have to take care of. My assistant is going to screen the calls for the show tonight."

Claire nodded. "All right."

Drew turned to Mark. "Let me know if there's anything I can do to help catch this guy. I'm tightening security. Claire will be escorted inside the building at all times."

"Yes, she will be," Mark said. "I don't intend to leave her alone for a second."

Drew nodded, then excused himself while his assistant, a lean college intern named Bailey, took over.

Claire walked into the sound room, then turned to Mark. "I have an idea. What if I invite the killer to call in and talk to me? You could trace—"

"No!" Mark snapped. "For God's sake, Claire, if you do that, you'll have every nut across the state phoning in."

"I don't want any more women to die, Mark." She reached for his arm, determined to convince him. "You said he's playing with me. Maybe the key to catching him is for me to play the game. I could trap him—"

"Absolutely not." Mark cut her off, unwilling to consider it. "It's too dangerous, Claire. Just have some faith in me, I'll find him."

THEY WOULD NEVER find him.

He traced a finger over the rose petal, the delicate tips that had once been bloodred but had now turned brown with death. Closing his eyes, he imagined them scattered across the white sand like ashes, the remnants of a fire that had been snuffed out before it had had a chance to burn.

Like Claire's feelings for him. If only he'd had more time with her. That would change soon.

But the others…they didn't deserve a second chance. They hadn't even bothered to be nice to him.

A ball of fury burst inside him, and he opened his eyes, crushing the rose in his fist. He had been so close to Claire earlier. Had brushed her skin with his fingertips, tasted the fear in the air that had been fraught with tension between them. He had wanted her to look up at him and smile, to whisper his name and know that he loved her.

Dropping the battered flower on the floorboard of his car, he reached for the silk scarf he'd taken from her dresser and slid it into his pocket, then opened the car door and stepped out. He checked his watch, his breathing quickening when his next victim appeared from the shadows of her beach cottage.

She was right on time.

He'd watched her for weeks. Knew every detail about her routine, her likes and dislikes.

She always took a moonlit walk along the beach. Alone. At night.

Unfortunately, this one would be her last.

Chapter Eight

Have faith in me, Claire.

She did have faith in Mark where his job was concerned, but she didn't believe he wanted an imperfect woman. Especially one who would be a burden and slow him down.

The signal buzzer dinged beneath her hand, and she startled, dragging herself back to work. When she'd first reviewed the list of topics for the show and realized tonight's program focused on lovers who'd returned from the past, she'd almost changed the agenda. But she'd organized her list of topics weeks ago and refused to let Mark's return alter her decisions regarding her work. After all, he had only reappeared in her life because of this case. When the police found the Midnight Murderer, he'd disappear again.

And this time when he walked away, she wanted her heart left intact.

The first two callers had suffered bitter breakups. In the first scenario, the husband had slept with the woman's best friend. In the second, the man had embezzled his wife's trust fund and absconded with all her jewels. Neither relationship could be salvaged, in Claire's estimation, so she'd encouraged the women to face the truth about the men they'd once loved and move on.

"Claire, I don't know what to do," the caller said. "Just last week, I thought I was finally over my old boyfriend, but he showed up at my door yesterday with flowers and an apology that was hard to turn down."

"How did your relationship end?" Claire asked.

"We were both young. I'd just graduated from high school, and he went off to college."

"How long has it been since you've seen him?"

"It's my third year of college now. He graduated and has a job in a computer company."

"Was there someone else at the time?" Claire asked.

"I don't think so."

"So, you parted because you both needed to grow up?"

"He wanted to date college girls," the girl said defensively. "He thought I was just a kid."

"You probably don't want to hear this, Annika, but you *were* just a kid. It sounds like he realized you both needed to explore life before settling down into a serious relationship."

"Well, yeah..."

"Are you involved with someone else now?"

"Sort of an on-again, off-again."

"Are you in love with the new guy, or do you still love your old boyfriend?"

The girl hesitated. "I think I'm still in love with my old boyfriend."

"Is your new boyfriend serious about you?"

"He…yeah, he seems to be."

"But you don't feel the same way."

"I've tried to, but I can't make myself feel romantic about him."

Claire nodded. "If you aren't in love with him, break it off. It's not fair to lead him on or keep him around for convenience sake."

Maybe that had been the reason Mark had let her go when she'd returned his ring. Thinking about leaving for his mission unattached had made him momentarily desperate, but once he'd shipped out, he'd realized he didn't really want to marry.

"I'm afraid that's true. I have kept Barry around because I was afraid of being alone."

"Being alone is scary, but women need to learn to depend on themselves, and love themselves. Then they'll have healthier relationships with men."

"You're right. My mom's done okay on her own."

"That a girl. If you still have feelings for your old boyfriend, and you believe he's sincere, maybe you should give him another chance."

"I do want to try," the girl said. "But I can't forget that he hurt me."

"No, but you can sort through the past together so you can move on. Leaving things unsettled may be holding you back from loving someone else. And if he's sincere, who knows?"

"You're right, I can't keep running scared." The girl thanked her and hung up.

Claire considered her own situation. Unfortunately,

she had yet to meet another man who stirred her desires and yearnings like Mark had. Was she holding on to the past? Unable to allow another man in her life because her heart still belonged to Mark? Had she been running scared the past year?

But she couldn't settle things between her and Mark without revealing the truth about the night she'd lost their baby.

And that was one truth she wasn't ready to disclose—it would be like tearing out her soul.

Now her future was even more uncertain—the killer might be targeting her as his next victim.

HAD CLAIRE thought of them when she'd been talking to the girl? Their past was fraught with problems. Him leaving. Now her accident.

Everything had changed. *He* had changed.

After all he had seen, after watching his fellow soldiers die and knowing that he should have been with them, he didn't deserve to have Claire.

Claire had changed, too.

She'd always been independent and strong, had been full of life, ready to take chances. She'd been caring but passionate. Now, she seemed remote, as if she'd accepted her plight and had devoted herself to her work. Her caring nature was evident, at least for her patients, but what had happened to her passion for life?

Still, even though she was vulnerable, she was determined not to rely on anyone. The very reason she'd moved to Savannah. Mark had to admire her tenacity and her ability to cope. And he still couldn't prevent the tide of desire that washed over him every time he was near her. It had nearly overcome him the first time he'd met her, and hadn't diminished during their time apart. Instead, it had grown in intensity, pounding inside him stronger and more earnest than ever. Sometimes he wasn't sure he could fight it any longer. But he should.

Claire had moved on. Why couldn't he?

Pushing his feelings aside, he phoned Detective Black while Claire kept the radio conversation flowing. Mark filled Black in on the earlier events. "You have the beaches staked out?"

"We put as much manpower on it as we can."

"Have you guys found a connection with the roses?"

"Devlin said Lassiter's name showed up. Apparently he grows his own roses. We're getting a warrant to check his property, and see if he might have grown the variety the killer is leaving."

Mark rubbed the bridge of his nose. That might be a break. "Good. I'll fax you a list of all the employees at the radio station," Mark said. "And I'll copy them to Agent Devlin, too."

"We'll check the database and see if any red flags pop up."

"I don't care if it's a misdemeanor, a complaint from a woman that was dropped, I want to know everything you find," Mark said. "This guy's getting bolder, showing up at Claire's workplace, following her home."

"That means he'll get sloppy, make a mistake," Black said. "Then we'll catch him."

Mark grunted, then hung up. They'd better catch

him before he got close to Claire again. If he laid one finger on her, Mark would kill him with his bare hands.

HIS HANDS tightened around the long stem of the rose as he plucked the petals and scattered them across the sand. The thorns bit into his fingers.

He welcomed the pain.

The sharp prickles distracted him from the fact that Claire had been offering advice to a young, silly girl, while all the time he'd heard the wistfulness in Claire's voice, as if she still wanted Mark Steele.

He had been so close to her earlier. Had brushed her hair. Had inhaled her evocative scent.

And he'd felt the fear emanate from her.

She knew he was strong. Whole. A man.

A man who wanted her.

A man who always got what he wanted.

Dropping the last petal onto the woman's buttermilk-pale skin, he removed the portable phone and punched in Claire's number. When her voice echoed over the line in welcome, he lifted his head and closed his eyes, pretending she was there beside him, reaching out her hand to soothe away the pain from the thorny needles.

And from the ones who had betrayed him. Like the woman lying dead in the sand.

"HELLO, THIS IS CLAIRE, you're on the air. Who am I speaking with?"

A low, throaty voice murmured, "Did you get the rose, Claire?"

Mark froze, then motioned to the assistant to substitute music for air time, make sure the trace was intact and that the phone call was on the private line so it wouldn't air. They didn't want to scare people even more. The citizens of Savannah were already frightened, and rightfully so.

"Yes," Claire said into the microphone. "But you didn't mention your name." She lowered her voice to a sultry pitch. "Tell me more about yourself."

Mark balled his hands into his fists. She was baiting the man, leading him on.

The caller made a husky tsking sound. "I love your sexy voice," he said, ignoring her question. "It makes me hard for you."

Mark fisted his hands.

"Why do you choose roses?" Claire asked, ignoring him this time. "Do they have a special meaning for you? Did your mother grow roses?"

"I don't want to talk about my mother, Claire. Now why aren't we on the air?"

"It's more intimate this way," Claire replied. "And why don't you want to talk about your mother? Didn't you two get along?"

"She died a long time ago," he said in a strained voice. "I barely remember her."

"I'm sorry, what happened to her?"

"I told you I don't want to talk about her."

"All right, but I'm still curious. Why roses?"

His breath hissed out. "Because they stand for love."

"The way your mother loved you?"

"She didn't love anyone but herself," he said, his voice rising with anger. "Just like the others."

"Tell me what others you're talking about. Is someone with you now?"

A shrill laugh crept over the line. "Not anymore. She was a bad girl." His voice grew menacing. "She had to be punished."

Claire dropped her head forward and closed her eyes as if she could obliterate his words. Mark ached to comfort her, but keeping the caller on the line was the best chance they had of locating him.

He also realized something else—this call wasn't prerecorded. But Drew wasn't manning the show. He could be anywhere in the building placing the call.

"What did she do that was so bad?" Claire asked.

"She ignored me, Claire. But you won't do that anymore, will you?"

Claire's jaw tightened. "No. I'd like to meet you, talk to you in person."

"Soon, Claire, very soon." He hesitated, his breathing filling the line just before the familiar song echoed from the caller, "Blinded by the light…"

"Let's meet right now. Tell me where," Claire said.

But the phone fell silent, the blare of the dial tone the only reply.

Mark grimaced. Dammit, they were too late.

Another woman was already dead.

CLAIRE YANKED the microphone closer to herself, and went back on air. "Excuse me, ladies and gentlemen, but I just received another call from the Midnight Murderer. If you're still listening, please phone back, talk to me. I know you want to tell me about yourself, about these women and the reason you're doing this." She paused, breathing deeply to control the panic in her voice. "This is Claire. I'm still here. I'm clearing the lines for your call."

She hesitated, waiting, hoping, but the buzzer remained silent. "Let me help you. You know it's wrong to kill these women, and you want me to help you stop. Please call back and let's talk."

A dead silence fell over the line. She gripped the microphone with sweaty palms, her pulse clamoring. "If it's me you want, then let the others go. I'll meet you anywhere you say."

The door to the room burst open, and footsteps hammered toward her. She didn't have to see him to know it was Mark. He was furious. She knew that. But she didn't care. She was desperate.

A strong, rough hand covered hers. Another grabbed the microphone away. Mark leaned over and whispered in her ear. "Sign off the show. *Now*, Claire."

She pushed his hand away and shook her head.

"He's not going to call again tonight. He's already gone."

The truth of his statement finally seeped through her consciousness. In her gut, she'd known the killer had dropped the phone the minute he'd hung up so he could escape, but she'd tried to reach out to him.

She nodded, swallowing to steady her voice, then leaned close to the microphone. "Ladies and gentlemen, if you have any information regarding the victims or this killer stalking our city, please contact the Savannah police." She recited the number for the hotline the police department had arranged with the FBI. "This is Dr. Claire Kos, signing off, and wishing you a pleasant night and a safe tomorrow."

Exhausted and shaking with tension, she dropped her head into her hands. Mark slid his hands beneath her arms, lifted her to stand, then pulled her against him, enveloping her into the sanctuary of his arms.

"We'll find him," Mark whispered into her hair.

Rage filled Claire. "When?" She tried to extricate herself from his embrace, but he held her tightly. "How many more women have to die before we stop him, Mark?"

"I don't know, but we will get him."

Tears pooled in her eyes, ready to fall, but she blinked them back. She hadn't cried since the night she'd lost her child. It was another sign of weakness she hated.

And now she felt so helpless, just as she had then.

"The police are combing the beaches now," Mark said in a low voice. "They had extra men out all night, maybe one of them is already onto something."

A labored breath escaped her. "But what if it's too late tonight? I'm not sure I can survive another woman's death on my conscience."

Mark hugged her closer, stroked her hair. "God, Claire, this isn't your fault."

"But he's calling me for a reason. Maybe he knows me, or wants to taunt me into catching him. I should pick up on something, some clue, and figure out who he is."

"You can't blame yourself, Claire. This sicko chose

you because you're in the public eye. It might not be personal at all."

Claire clutched his shirt. "You don't really believe that, Mark. The fact that he sent me the rose and came into my home, that seems more personal."

"He's getting too confident, taking chances, which means he'll slip up and we'll catch him."

Mark's cell phone rang, and he answered it. Feeling bereft without his comforting arms around her, she sagged back into the chair.

"Steele here." Claire sensed the tension radiating from Mark in the long pause that followed. "All right, I'll be right there."

She heard the snap of his phone closing, then he cleared his throat. "I have to go. I'll arrange for security to drop you at your place, Claire, and stay with you until I return."

Dread filled her, but she had to know the truth. "That was the police, wasn't it? They found another woman's body?"

Mark reached for her hand, then pressed it in his own. "I'm afraid so."

Claire stood. "Then I'm going with you."

"Claire, no—"

"Don't argue, Mark. Like you said, this madman is getting bolder. He's not waiting as long in between murders." She reached for her cane. "Maybe there'll be something at the scene to clue me into his identity. Then we can find him and make him pay for what he's done."

Mark hesitated. "All right, Claire, but you have to stay close to me. Is that understood?"

She nodded, and he slid his hand to her waist and guided her to the door. Claire started to refuse, but the contact felt so heavenly that she didn't bother to protest. For once, she allowed herself the sanctuary of his comfort.

Too soon, Mark would be gone again, and she would be fighting the world all on her own.

"WHERE ARE WE?" Claire asked.

"Tybee Island." Mark parked, circled around to the passenger side, but Claire had already opened the door and was climbing out. "Here, take my arm."

She hesitated, and he sensed she hated this part of her dependence.

"It's rocky," he said, pacing his longer gait to match hers. "And we're going down a slight hill."

She nodded and inched along beside him. He steered them through a patch of sea oats, but she nearly stumbled over a plastic shovel left in the sand, and he steadied her.

"Sorry, I should have warned you."

She tensed, and he covered her hand with his. "I'll get the hang of this, Claire. I promise."

"You don't have to get the hang of it," Claire said. "You'll be gone soon and it won't matter."

"It'll always matter," he said in a gruff voice, his emotions more on the surface than he'd realized. God, she was so beautiful with the moonlight spilling across her golden hair. "*You'll* always matter."

Claire froze, and he squeezed her hand, but a noise interrupted the moment.

"The police are up ahead," Mark murmured. "They're already working the crime scene."

"You'll have to be my eyes, Mark. And please don't leave out anything to spare me. A detail might make the difference in saving another woman's life."

Or saving hers, Mark realized. "All right."

Detective Black met them as they approached. "It looks like the same guy."

"Have you identified the victim yet?"

"Not yet. She's a white female, probably early thirties, redhead."

"Signs of a struggle?"

"Some. Her clothes are slightly torn, although there's no visible signs of rape. The M.E. will tell us more."

"Can I see her?" Mark asked.

"Sure, but don't touch anything, and stay behind the tape."

Mark nodded and led Claire nearer the body.

Claire's hand tightened around Mark's hand. "What do you see?"

"She's lying facedown like the others, her arms are stretched above her head. The crushed rose is in her right hand."

"Anything else?"

"She was strangled with a scarf," Detective Black said.

Mark stiffened. "Let's see it."

Black walked over and took an evidence bag from the crime-scene officer, then brought it back and held it up.

"Describe it," Claire said.

"It's mostly black with a lime green design running through it," Mark said. "I can't read the label."

"We can probably trace the store where it came from," Detective Black said. "Although the first two were cheap discount store brands. This one is silk."

"It came from the Pelican," Claire said.

"How do you know?" Detective Black asked.

"Because the scarf is mine."

IN SPITE OF the oppressive heat, a cold chill permeated Claire, her stomach a bundle of knots. "Can I please get closer to the woman?"

"If you think it might do some good," Detective Black said. "But let me check with CSU first."

Black walked away and Mark growled. "He used the scarf he stole from your house to kill now. That's way too personal."

Claire folded her arms across her middle. "I know. I'm trying to put it together, profile what he's doing."

Black returned and led her to the woman. Claire stooped down, and Mark moved beside her. "Is there anything distinctive about her?" Claire asked.

"No tattoos, body piercings or other injuries."

"She doesn't look like either of the other victims?"

"No, I don't see a pattern. At least not as far as body type, hair color or size. He must be choosing random victims."

"I don't think so. He plans it out. He's probably watched them for a while, learned their routine and habits. There's something we're missing." Claire leaned forward, the scent of death assaulting her. But another smell permeated the air, it had caught in the evening breeze. "There's that odor again. I can't figure out what it is."

"What odor?" Mark asked.

"I'm not sure," Claire said. "I can't put my finger on it, but it smells like some kind of antibiotic cream. Tell the M.E. to check it out. Maybe it's a topical ointment for a rash or skin disorder. Identifying it might help us find the killer."

"When did you smell it before?"

"When he came into my house, and then on the stairwell."

"Then this is definitely the same guy." Mark cleared his throat. "And you're right, identifying it might help us find the killer."

Claire fell silent, the implications of it all swirling around in her head.

"What is it, Claire?"

She stood, and he ushered her back across the sand a safe distance from the scene.

"I was thinking about the rose," Claire said. "If the red one means love, the dead one must mean his love for these women is dead or their love for him was dead. Maybe it never blossomed at all. He must have met them somewhere before or known them somehow."

"That makes sense," he mumbled. "But that means he's in love with you."

Claire fought a shudder. An image of this crazed man holding her scarf, wrapping it around his hands, then the woman's throat, flashed into her head. But why her? How did she know him?

"Don't worry," he murmured. "We're in this together, Claire."

She lifted her face to the wind. "Are we, Mark?"

He gripped her arms. "You're damn right we are. Any more ideas?"

"About my scarf? Yes." Claire hesitated. "Using it to kill means he's killing because of me. Maybe he wants the victims to be me, or at least to look like me in death."

Which meant she was going to be his ultimate victim.

Chapter Nine

He was coming after Claire.

Mark knew it without a doubt now. And he had to stop him.

He glanced at Claire, hating the look of guilt on her face as if she could somehow have prevented this madman's spree of killing. She settled into his car, her hands wrapped around her arms as if she was physically trying to hold herself together.

He lifted a hand, caressed her chin with the pad of his thumb. "Claire, this isn't your fault."

She tensed. "Then why are all these things connected to me?"

"I don't know…yet."

She chewed her bottom lip in concentration. "There's something about me that triggered this man's hatred of women. Either I did something to him personally, or I represent the type of woman who once hurt him. It might be my job. Maybe his mother was a psychologist or a counselor. Or maybe he wanted to date me and I turned him down, or he thought I would, and he was too afraid to ask…if I only knew what it was…."

He started the car and drove into the street. Unfortunately, she was right, but that didn't make her responsible. Of course, he understood about irrational feelings of guilt. No matter how many times he told himself there was nothing he could have done to save his men, he still felt the weight of their deaths on his conscience. At night, when he closed his eyes, he saw their faces, white and wide-eyed, filled with the realization that they were going to die.

It was past time to help them.

But he would find a way to save Claire. And the only way to do that was to catch the maniac before he took another life.

He'd see what the locals had learned about Lassiter's rose garden, and if the M.E. identified the cream or ointment the killer used. At this point, they needed concrete clues.

"I'll look over the data I collected on the employees when I get back to your place." He checked to see if anyone was following them, but the road seemed empty, the night sounds of the ocean drifting through the open window. The air felt humid, too, the stars obliterated by dark clouds, adding shadows to the overhang of trees bordering the narrow road.

Claire nodded. "And I'll review my patient files again tomorrow."

"Do you have a suspect in mind?"

Claire shrugged. "Two of my patients fit the profile, but I have no definitive reason to name either of them."

Claire leaned her head back and closed her eyes, and he realized that was her way of ending the discussion.

Frustration filled him. Tomorrow, he'd talk to Black about the possibility of issuing a court order to force Claire to disclose her files. She wouldn't like it, but he didn't care. He had to protect her, even if she fought him every step of the way.

Five minutes later he parked in her driveway, and they went inside.

"I'm going to check out your place," Mark said.

"Does it look as if someone's been here?"

"No, but we aren't taking any chances. Wait here."

Hands clasped together, Claire nodded and waited in the small living room until he searched the cottage, and returned. "All clear."

Claire sighed in relief. "Thanks for the ride, Mark. I'll see you later."

"I'm not going anywhere."

She paused, one slender hand on the wall leading to her bedroom. "What?"

Although fear laced her voice, and stubbornness, too, shadows from the window danced around her, painting an erotic glow. "I'm sleeping on your couch."

"But, Mark—"

"He's killed three women." Mark reached for her, needing to touch her. "He's been inside your cottage once. He may come again. And if he does, I intend to be here and catch him." The image of this latest dead women had been frozen in his mind—the strangle marks on her neck, the way her head had been twisted at an odd angle, her face turned down into the sand as if, even in death, she should be ashamed. And there was Claire's scarf...

His mind flashed to an image of Claire lying in the woman's place—Claire's hair spread on the sand, her body limp, the bloodred rose petals fluttering around her. He went cold inside. Perspiration dotted his forehead as he cupped her face in his hands. "God, Claire, when I saw that woman tonight, all I could think of was that it might have been you."

Claire's breath hitched in her throat. "M-maybe it was supposed to be me instead of them."

"No." A dull ache ripped at his chest. "Don't say that. Don't even think it."

"But—"

"I won't let him get his hands on you, Claire." He stroked her cheeks with his fingers, his voice gruff. "I'll stay with you here or take you to a safe house."

"I...I need to be here."

Because she was blind, comfortable in her surroundings? Or because she was daring the killer to come after her?

For a brief second, her voice sounded so tiny and fragile, as if fear had stolen her stubborn independence, just as it had robbed him of his own common sense. Selfish as it was, he was grateful the dead woman wasn't Claire. He needed to feel that she was alive.

He drew her to him, lowered his head, traced her lips with his finger. She hesitated slightly, then responded with a breathy whisper of his name. He pressed his lips over hers and crushed her against him. How many times had he lain awake in the desert and imagined he'd heard that voice calling his name in the lonely darkness of the night? How many times had he dreamt of touching her one more time?

She tasted like sweetness and strength with a hint of vulnerability and the saucy desire that had always made her unique. And her slender body was alive in his hands, making his heart pound.

He struggled for control, and ordered himself to stop, but he had an empty place inside that only Claire could fill, and he deepened the kiss, tracing her lips with his tongue until she parted and welcomed him inside. His pulse racing, he slid one hand into the curly strands of her hair, then slid the other to her waist, brought her body up against him.

His need flared, hot and burning beyond control, and he cupped her bottom and moved his leg in between her thighs. Sheer hunger drove him on, and he rubbed against her belly until she groaned and responded. Her nipples stiffened beneath her shirt, her breasts tortured his own flat chest, and temptation urged him to undress her, then touch and taste her all over. Shifting so she could feel his burgeoning weight against the heat of her, he growled and explored her mouth, boldly telling her how much he still wanted her.

A broken engagement and the devastation of war hadn't lessened the intensity of his desire.

But Claire pulled away, trying to compose herself. "Why are you doing this, Mark?"

His breath came out a ragged reply. "Because I still want you, Claire. I think that's obvious."

She shook her head. "No…it's over."

"You can't say that, Claire, not after that kiss."

Claire's expression turned pained. A tear escaped her eye and rolled down her cheek. "But…it's too late."

He grabbed her arm and pulled her back to him. "That's not true. We can make it work."

"I'm not the same person I used to be, Mark," Claire argued. "And neither are you."

"Maybe not," he said gruffly. "But the heat is still there." He rubbed himself against her. "You feel it, Claire. Just admit it. Say you want me."

An agonized whisper tore from her throat. "Stop it, Mark. That isn't fair—"

"And it's fair that you're blind?" His voice grew hard. "And some maniac is stalking you?"

She trembled against him. "No, none of it is fair, but that's the way it is. You left to do a job, to fight for our country—"

"Is that what this is about?" His hands tightened around her arm. "Dammit, I did leave, but I'm back now, Claire, and I'm not going anywhere."

"You're in the FBI. You'll be leaving all the time to work on cases." Her voice broke. "You'll be in danger, going undercover, working with all sorts of evil people and criminals. Who's to say that when you go to work in the morning that you'll come back at night?"

His temper deflated. All along he'd worried that his career had been part of the reason she hadn't shown that day. Now, he knew his work still bothered her. It would always bother her.

Still, he knew they could make it work. The old Claire wasn't like his mother. She was a fighter….

Unable to help himself, he pressed his lips against hers one more time. "Life can be extinguished in a minute, Claire. Nobody can promise tomorrow. We have to take everything we can get when we can get it."

Emotions clouded her face as she shook her head. "But you don't have to settle," Claire said.

"Is that what you think I'd be doing? Settling...because you're blind?"

Claire tried to pull away. "I...I can't do this right now, Mark. There's too much going on."

"Can't do what? Make love to me? Admit that you might need someone?" He wanted to shake her. "I need you, Claire." He sighed when she closed her eyes to shut him out. "There, I admitted it. Why can't you?"

She swayed toward him, the fire between them hotter than ever, but the distance was still there. And he didn't know how to reach her.

"Let me go." Her guttural plea tore at him.

Maybe he was wrong. Maybe she didn't love him. Maybe he was the only needy one....

"I'm sorry, Mark..." She turned and stumbled toward the hall, swinging her hands in a wide sweep to feel her way as if his kiss, his confession, had totally disoriented her.

His heart ached, seeing her that way.

Dammit. He wanted her back. The old Claire. The one who looked at him with passion and desire, not the one who ran from his touch.

And he'd give anything to restore her sight. Maybe then she'd accept him back into her life.

He had to find out more about her condition. She

hadn't mentioned whether surgery was an option, a corneal transplant maybe…

But what if she never saw again? Could they possibly be together anyway?

He wanted to chase after her, reassure her that everything was all right, that he would always take care of her, but Claire didn't want to be taken care of. So he fisted his hands by his sides and reminded himself that the case had to take priority.

After that, he had no idea what would happen. He had walked away from Claire once, and let her go.

He damn sure wouldn't walk away this time without a fight.

CLAIRE STRIPPED OUT OF her clothes and threw on a nightgown, her body still humming with desire for Mark. The moment he'd touched her, she'd nearly fallen apart in his arms. She felt like a starved woman craving food, and the only man who could feed that hunger was the man in the other room sacked out on her couch.

She remembered his preference for sleeping in the nude and wondered if he was peeling off his clothes that moment, stripping out of his jeans and allowing his body to breathe the night air. In her mind's eye, she saw the dark hair that had dusted his chest and the muscles that had bulged in his arms when he'd risen above her. His eyes had turned smoky when he'd slid inside her, then darkened to coal-black when he'd begun to pump harder. And his scent, the smell of a man driven by need and want, a man filled with lust who liked to take but who always satisfied her cravings before his own.…

She would never be satisfied, not without him.

Shutting out the thoughts that she could not have him again, she curled into a ball on her side, willing the ache to cease, but she could almost feel his hands on her bare body, stroking her inner thigh, teasing her legs apart, his mouth suckling her breasts while his fingers delved deeper and deeper inside her. Teasing. Exploring. Magically bringing alive every sensation that had lain dormant in his absence. Spinning a web of desire so intricate that she would plead for him to take her to heaven and help her see the light.

She rolled to her stomach and punched the pillow. Back to reality. She lived in a world of darkness, a world she had brought on herself.

She deserved no better.

A summer breeze fluttered the trees outside, and the branches spattered softly against the window. Sweat trickling down her back, she rose and opened the window, allowing the evening air to cool her. But the grating low voice of the killer echoed through the shadows of the trees. He was calling her name.

Bad girls have to be punished, Claire. But you're not a bad girl, are you?

His words taunted her with the truth of her secrets. Yes, she was a bad girl.

Her mother had constantly chided her on being bad when she was little. Her sister was the good child, the well-behaved one. Claire had been mischievous. She'd even gotten into scraps at school. Although she'd been standing up for friends who were targets of bullies, her mother wanted the perfect, sweet, docile child. The one who wore leotards and tights, played with china dolls. The teenager who aspired to be the perfect tennis-club wife.

She had never been docile or sweet. She'd never wanted to be a tennis-club wife.

And she certainly wasn't perfect now. She never would be.

Really, she never had been. She'd let her selfish needs drive her to chase Mark. She'd hoped he'd look into her eyes at the airport, declare his love and not say goodbye.

Did the killer know her secrets? Was that why he'd called her to taunt her about the others?

Mark's face materialized in her mind, and she glanced back at the bedroom door, wondering if he was asleep. She ached to go to him and curl up in his arms, feel his heat next to her, inside her, replacing the cold. She wanted to forget the nightmares for one night.

But how could she make love to him with secrets still between them?

Instead she crawled back into bed and stared into the black emptiness that represented her life.

IT WAS DARK OUTSIDE. No moon. Their mission was almost over. They'd been successful so far. And soon the unit would be disbanded. Everyone would return to their own lives.

They had so much to look forward to.

Abe would go back to his wife and child.

Odd, how he and Abe had gotten so close in such a short time. But that was what war did to a man.

Especially when he was alone.

Mark fought the bitterness of knowing he had no place to go, no place to call home, no one to welcome him back from battle.

Unlike Abe. He was once again showing off photos of his son, and his beautiful wife. Mark stared at the pictures with envy.

Then a noise rumbled in the distance. Thunder? A tank? Another noise. Footsteps.

All the men jumped to alert, stomping out the campfire, grabbing weapons and canvassing the area.

Today they had celebrated a victory battle. But tonight had been quiet.

Too quiet.

Mark should have known.

Suddenly, all hell broke loose. A grenade exploded in front of him. Mark jumped for cover, but the explosion caught two of his men. Fire exploded. Then another explosion. And another. He darted behind the army jeep, his heart racing, dirt, sand, debris from the explosion swirling around him. The scent of death floated toward him.

One of his men was on fire. Another bleeding. Another jerking as death claimed him.

He searched the darkness, opened fire, never saw the storm of men coming.

Seconds later, the entire camp was in ashes. The bloody bodies of his men lay piled among the burning embers.

Abe stretched out his hand, reached for Mark. He tried to drag him from the fire. But Mark could hardly *move. He'd been hit in the leg, his gut torn open, and he was shot in the shoulder. His lungs burned as he dragged himself forward. Pain knifed through his stomach, rippled up his lungs. Blood oozed from his lips, ran from his shoulder. His fingers clawed at the dirt, raking the parched sand. But just as he reached his buddy, Abe's eyes widened in horror. He had his dog tags in his hand.*

"Tell Marie I love her, and Kevin, tell him I love him, too. Give him this."

Mark's throat choked as Abe whispered his name. He couldn't die. Abe was getting ready to go home. To play ball with his son. Take him to his first soccer practice.

Then his buddy's outstretched hand went limp, his mouth parted. Blood gurgled from his nose and mouth. His dog tags fell into the sand.

"Noooo!"

Mark jerked awake, his lungs tight, his body shaking. Disoriented, he searched the darkness. For Abe. For his other men.

But they were all dead.

And he was in Savannah. At Claire's.

He dropped his head into his hands, sweating profusely. He couldn't let Claire die, too. No, he couldn't live if that happened.

FRUSTRATED and still dressed, he threw himself off the couch, flipped on a light to shut out the grisly images of his men and paced the room. Dammit, it was all so unfair. Abe's wife and son left behind. The other men and their futures destroyed.

He couldn't let it happen to Claire.

Knowing he couldn't go back to sleep, he retrieved all the files on the male employees at CIRP and on the station manager. Swiping a hand through his sweat-soaked hair, he reviewed them.

Ian Hall had come on board as Director of CIRP a few months ago when Arnold Hughes had disappeared. Hughes had created the trouble with unethical experimentation and research, which had given the research center a bad name, and Hall was here to expunge it. But Ian Hall had been acquainted with Hughes and the original founders of CIRP, had been their colleague twenty-plus years ago when he was a research doctor himself. According to the information Devlin and the Savannah P.D. had gathered, Hall had worked with genetic engineering in the pioneer stages. In the early eighties, several years of his life hadn't been accounted for, which gave Mark pause. A red flag waved, and he made a note to check it out. Even if the missing information didn't pertain to this case, it might prove interesting to the files on CIRP and the special projects the FBI were investigating. What exactly had Hall been working on back then?

On a more personal note, he saw that Hall had been married early in his career, and divorced for several years. He had no children, had been raised in a modest home, but his parents had been educated. No mention of childhood abuse or trauma, which didn't mean he couldn't be a killer, but he didn't fit the profile, either.

He glanced at the next file. George Ferguson had been raised in Florida, attended Duke University, then

Cornell. His father had apparently died in a boating accident when George was young. His mother was a psychologist in North Carolina. Hmm. Claire had mentioned that the killer might relate to someone in her profession. And Ferguson had been alone the night of the second murder. He would check with Black tomorrow to see if he and the others had an alibi for this last one. If he hadn't been questioned, Mark would pay a visit himself.

And now Kurt Lassiter. He frowned. The man definitely had an interest in Claire. He grew roses. Mark called Black. "Did you check out that rose garden yet?"

"Yes, but Lassiter's into some exotic varieties. None match the standard roses found at the crime scenes."

"Meaning he probably would have chosen something more unusual to leave with the victims."

"Probably."

Mark thanked him and hung up, although he still couldn't eliminate Lassiter. The man was smart. Perhaps he'd ingeniously used a common rose to throw them off. Maybe he'd even done so for symbolic reasons—he felt the women weren't significant, they weren't worth a rare, special variety.

Man, he was beginning to sound like Claire.

And Lassiter's ex-girlfriend had died a suspicious death. He skimmed further into the file. Lassiter's father was a miner, his mother a housekeeper. Kurt Lassiter was obviously the overachiever. Perhaps he even resented his working-class roots.

No record of abuse was listed although a small notation mentioned some kind of bike accident and head trauma when he was a teenager. There were no details on the incident, but from his own medical background, Mark knew that physical trauma could trigger psychotic breaks or episodes that might not reveal themselves until later. He'd have to look into it. Or ask Claire.

Right. Like she wanted him treating her friend as a suspect.

Exhausted and well aware it was already near morning, he decided to try and get some shut-eye. One look at her sofa warned him it was too small for him, but it would have to do.

Claire would not welcome him in her bed tonight.

He unbuttoned his oxford shirt and tossed it over the back of the desk chair, then slid off his jeans, stripping down to his boxers. At home, he would strip those, too, but just in case trouble happened, it was best he keep them on. Then a low sound rumbled from Claire's bedroom, and he paused and listened. There it was again.

His heart jumping, he checked his gun, then crept toward the bedroom to search for the source. He eased open the bedroom door and saw the curtain fluttering from the open window.

Fear slammed into him. Had someone snuck inside?

THE PHONE CALLS weren't enough. And neither were the other women.

They weren't Claire.

They didn't have her smile. Her soft, sultry voice. The compassion he saw in her sightless eyes.

He wanted to see her in person. To breathe the air near her face. To touch the silky strands of her hair.

Only then would he feel alive.

He had been breathing in her sight through the window, but the door swung open and he ducked low, then crept back through the sea oats flanking the small lot. Damn, Mark Steele was at her place, spending the night.

A jealous rage balled inside his stomach, burning a path through his gut, and he headed down the grassy embankment to the beach with the wind whipping by his side.

At least Steele had not been in her bed.

But he was ensconcing himself in her life as if he had a right.

He broke into a dead run, the sand kicking behind him, trampling shells that shattered beneath his feet until he was a good two miles down from her cottage, all the way to the base of Serpent's Cove where he'd taken his first victim. His leg throbbed, and he paused to rub the knotted muscle, cursing his weakness.

Then he dropped onto the wet sand and let the dampness seep into his back. The dark smell of death wafted from the sharp jagged rocks of the cove and the ledge above, and he stared up at the starless night in search of the moon. Remembering the man he once had been only drove the pain of whom he'd become deeper, like the blade of a serrated knife. Anguish robbed his breath, and he closed his eyes. With Claire, he could still be that perfect man. Yes, Claire would see beneath the surface, she could love the man that lay within.

But frustration for all he had lost mounted inside him, as well as the unfairness that Mark Steele should be sleeping in her house tonight instead of him. Steele had deserted her when she'd needed him most. He didn't deserve to be with her tonight or any other time.

The incessant itching on his skin began to prick at him like needles, and he clawed at the red, puffy skin. He would make it worse, he knew, but he couldn't handle the pain. Not of being without Claire and his own ill-gotten fate. Tears rained down his face as he raised his head and released a long, anguished cry. He hated them all, Mark Steele, the government, the people at CIRP, the women who'd rebuked him—they had done this to him and they had to pay.

A second later, the pitiful sound of his cries echoed into the night, then caught in the wind and floated out to sea and the rolling tides.

Chapter Ten

Claire doubled over and began to sob. "No, it's my fault. Leave me…just let me die."

Mark froze at the bedroom door. Claire was thrashing about as if she was fighting someone, her gulping breaths sounding agonized. What was she dreaming about? The murders? Her accident?

"No…please…I can't see…"

He hurriedly checked through the window, but no one was there. Then a shadow moved in the distance. It might be nothing. Or it might be the killer. Part of him wanted to chase it down, but he couldn't leave Claire alone. Not when she was crying from the depths of a nightmare.

And if he left and the killer was watching, he might come in.

"No…"

Mark catapulted forward, dropped onto the bed beside her and pulled her into his arms. "Shh, Claire, wake up, honey, it's a dream, just a dream." He stroked her hair and back, murmuring nonsensical words to her and cradling her in his arms, until she finally opened her eyes. Even then, she couldn't escape the never-ending darkness that trapped her in its clutches.

He understood all about the darkness. The nightmares that couldn't be escaped.

"I'm here now, Claire, I'm sorry I wasn't there before, but I'm here now."

Another low sob ripped from deep within her throat, tearing at his insides.

"Shh, baby, let me hold you. It's all right."

She curled into his embrace and pressed her damp cheeks against his bare chest. He shouldn't have taken such pleasure in the gesture, but it had been so long since he'd held a woman in his arms. And not just any woman. Claire.

There had been no one since her.

He wasn't sure if there ever would be again.

Tightening his embrace, he swayed back and forth with her in his arms. "Tell me about your nightmare."

She shook her head and his jaw went rigid.

"We once shared things, Claire. Our goals in life, our bodies. Can't you share your bad dreams with me now?"

She wiped at her teary eyes, and he ached again for her. "I…was dreaming about the killer."

But she'd been pleading to die.

"Not about your accident?"

She stiffened and started to pull away, but he held her tight. "Please talk to me, Claire. It'll make things better."

"No, it…nothing will help."

Because he couldn't erase the darkness? Just like he hadn't been able to save Abe. "Then let me hold you tonight."

She nodded slightly, her silence reminding him of the chasm that yawned between them, but they stretched back on the bed together. She snuggled into his arms, and he cradled her head in the crook of his shoulder, stroking her hair and murmuring soothing sounds until her body slowly relaxed. An eternity later, her breathing finally settled into the steady rhythm of sleep.

He dropped a kiss into her hair, then wound the satiny strands around his hand and wrapped his legs around hers, holding her tightly. Suddenly gaining her trust meant everything to him, even more than the case. More than his job.

Tomorrow, he would find out what he could about her accident and what had caused it. And soon he would get her to open up to him. Then maybe he could help erase her pain and make up for everything the killer had put her through.

CLAIRE WOKE, nestled inside Mark's comforting arms, his breath tickling the top of her head. It was the first time she'd felt safe in months.

Don't get too dependent, Claire. He won't be around for long.

Memories of the night before, of finding the third murder victim and talking to the killer haunted her. But she hadn't been dreaming about the killer; she'd been dreaming about the accident and losing her baby. She hadn't said anything in her sleep, had she?

She inhaled Mark's masculine scent and wondered if he could possibly forgive her if he knew the truth.

But why bother him with what could never be? He'd be leaving as soon as they found the Midnight Murderer.

"You're beautiful in the morning."

Claire startled. She hadn't known Mark was awake. Could he read the truth on her face?

She detested being at such a disadvantage.

"I need to get ready for work."

He caught her arm before she could slide off the bed. "Are you sure you don't want to hide out here today? I could keep you company."

"And how would you explain that to the feds?"

A low chuckle rumbled from his chest, a sound she had once treasured because it had been so rare. "That I was playing bodyguard." His finger trailed down her spine, then lower, seductive. "You know I don't mind guarding your body."

Claire's breath caught, the hint of desire lacing his voice automatically resurrecting her own hunger for him. Mark had always been affectionate in the morning.

But she couldn't see his face or his eyes, so she had no idea if pity, guilt or simple proximity triggered his comment or if he truly still had feelings for her.

Then he lowered his mouth and brushed his lips across hers, tempting, teasing, stoking the simmering fire burning between them. Claire couldn't resist. Forgetting all the reasons she shouldn't succumb to his touch, she met his need with her own, sliding her hands up to press against his cheek. She had loved his strong jaw, the hard military set to his expression, the barely controlled passion he exuded.

Now she desperately needed to taste that passion.

His tongue danced inside her mouth while his fingers skimmed down her waist, then lower to pluck at the hem of her gown and inch beneath the thin fabric. Her skin heated to a fever pitch and she moaned, digging her hands into his hair and deepening the kiss. Then he was cupping her bottom, rolling his hips forward, tangling his legs with hers until she lay prisoner to his command.

MARK WANTED to take Claire with a fierceness that bordered on primal. One touch to her thigh, and he felt her body shimmy with want. His own sex surged hard and potent, begging for release in the sweet haven of her body.

But the telephone jangled, jarring them both from the moment. "It might be the killer," Claire whispered.

"Calling your home phone?" Rage replaced his hunger. "It damn well better not be."

Claire's lip trembled as he pulled away. She started to reach for it, but he was closer. If the call was from the killer, he wanted to talk to him.

"Hello," he said into the receiver.

"Hello, who is this?"

Mark closed his eyes and released Claire. It was Claire's spoiled little sister. "Hello, Paulette."

"Mark?"

"Yes, it's me."

"What the hell are you doing there?"

Paulette had never liked him, but at least in the past she had been cordial.

"I'm working with the FBI."

"Listen, Mark, stay away from Claire," Paulette said sharply. "The last thing she needs right now is for you to drop in, turn her life upside down, then run out on her again."

Mark clenched his jaw. "In case you haven't seen the news lately, your sister's life has already been turned upside down, and not by me. I'm trying to protect her."

"And who's going to protect her from you?"

Her remark stabbed at his conscience. "You know a killer has been calling her."

"That's the reason I phoned. I want her to get out of town, to come stay with me."

For once they agreed on something. "That's a good idea."

"Let me talk to her," Claire said, reaching for the handset.

Paulette's words echoed in Mark's ears as he handed Claire the phone. Why was Paulette so bitter toward him? He'd proposed to Claire. It wasn't as if Claire had missed or wanted him enough to even write to him overseas. She seemed to have gotten over him…except she had responded to him in bed a moment ago. Because she was frightened.

Did Paulette think he'd known about her vision loss? Exactly when *had* Claire's accident occurred?

More questions assaulted him—questions he would find the answers to today.

"Paulette, hey, is everything all right?" Claire slipped on her robe and headed to the kitchen for some privacy.

"You tell me. What's *he* doing there?"

"Mark told you he's with the FBI. He's investigating the Midnight Murderer case."

"I don't mean that, Claire. What's he doing at your house this early in the morning?" Paulette's voice held derision. "You're not sleeping with him, are you?"

Claire hesitated, remembering the way she'd almost succumbed to temptation moments ago. How could Paulette understand her needs when she had the perfect life? When she methodically planned out every moment, event and friend to her specifications and never did anything impulsive?

"Claire?"

"No, we're not sleeping together," she whispered, "not that it's any of your business."

"It is my business. I had to help pick up the pieces after he deserted you, and when you were in the hospital facing a life without sight." Paulette sighed. "And let's not forget the child you were carrying."

Anger mushroomed inside her. "Mark never knew I was in the hospital."

"For God's sake, Claire, don't be idiotic and defend him. He didn't know because you wouldn't let me call him."

"I didn't want him to come back because he felt sorry for me," Claire cried.

"And you think he would have come running back?"

Claire hesitated. Had she wondered the same thing? Hadn't she trusted his love? Maybe that had been the problem, too. Footsteps sounded behind her, and she inhaled Mark's scent as he entered the kitchen. How much of her conversation had he overheard?

"Don't worry, Paulette. He's here to help catch the killer. We're not involved."

Mark cleared his throat behind her, and she knew he had heard her last comment. But they both needed reminding where they stood.

"I'm worried about that psycho on the loose, too," Paulette said. "It's bad enough you work with them, but now you have one stalking you."

"Paulette—"

"Why won't you come to Atlanta? I can hire someone to stay with you at my house. I have state-of-the-art security."

Claire fumed. Paulette thought money could buy everything. "I don't need a baby-sitter, Paulette. I may be able to help the police find this killer, and if I can, I intend to do so."

"But I don't want to see you hurt again, Claire, and I know Mark Steele will do that."

"Only if I allow it," Claire said, choosing her words carefully. "Now, I need to get dressed for work. I have patients to see."

"Don't go, Claire. For once in your life stop being so stubborn and independent. Come to Atlanta. Let the police handle the case."

"I can't do that," Claire said, knowing Paulette would never understand. "I have to help save these women."

"Saving them won't bring back your baby."

Claire bit her lip, her sister's words hitting her like a sharp blow.

A tense silence stretched between them, then her sister finally sighed. "I'm sorry, Claire. Call me if you change your mind, and I'll send someone to pick you up." Paulette's voice wobbled. "I know we don't always see eye to eye, but I do love you."

Claire paused, her own throat thick. Paulette meant well, but Claire had sensed her sister's disquietude about Claire's condition from the first moment Paulette had walked in the hospital room. Claire refused to be a burden or an embarrassment to anyone. And imperfection was considered an embarrassment to her sister just as it had been to her mother. "I love you, too, Paulette. I'll call you later."

She hung up and started the coffeemaker, then turned, but met the hard wall of Mark's chest.

"She's right, you know. You should stay with her."

"That's not going to happen," Claire said.

"Why not?"

"The last thing I want is to deal with Paulette now, Mark. End of subject."

His hands gently cupped her arms. "Your sister hates me, doesn't she?"

Claire sighed and fumbled with her robe. "Paulette means well. She's just trying to protect me."

"And she thinks I'll hurt you?" he asked in a gruff voice.

Claire couldn't deny the truth. "I don't want your pity, Mark, or my sister's."

He captured her hand and placed it over his chest,

then moved it lower. His erection surged against her, hard and pulsing full of life. "Make no mistake, Claire, my feelings for you, this need between us," he said in a husky voice, "it has nothing to do with pity."

Claire inhaled sharply. She could undress him right here in the kitchen, cradle his bulging sex in her hand, mount him on the floor, then slide his length inside her aching heat. They could extinguish the fire they'd started earlier, then build another one, long and slow and hot.

Mark could make her whole again… at least for a little while.

But her sister's warning rang in her head, followed by her own declaration that he couldn't hurt her unless she allowed it.

Seizing the curtains with what little resistance she had left and drawing them closed around her heart, she let her hand fall, then turned and darted into her bedroom for a shower. If the cost of loving Mark meant he'd find out about their lost child, then she had to walk away. To spare him the pain.

She'd face her problems alone.

AN HOUR LATER, Mark escorted Claire to her office, the tension between them palpable. He had let her escape to the shower earlier, but unfinished business lingered between them. Business and feelings that he realized they had to deal with or neither of them would be able to move on. Yet…

Could they possibly make their relationship work again? Fight the darkness together? Could she love him once more?

Did he deserve her love?

He headed to Ian Hall's office, deciding to kill two birds with one stone. He'd question Hall as to his whereabouts the night before, then ask him what he knew about Claire's accident and medical condition.

Hall was in a meeting, so he waited in the outer office, still troubled with Claire's sister's animosity toward him. He was trying to focus on the case when Hall returned and escorted him into his office.

"Agent Steele, I hope you're here to tell me you've found the Midnight Murderer."

Mark arched a brow. "Actually I came to ask if you have an alibi for last night."

Hall's jaw snapped tight. "I had a dinner party at my house for two scientists we're recruiting. There were at least twenty people there."

"What time did the party break up?"

"The last guest left about one o'clock in the morning."

Mark frowned. "Were Dr. Ferguson and Dr. Lassiter at the party?"

"Yes, both of them were."

"What time did they leave?"

"I don't remember. But you can't honestly tell me you believe one of them is a serial killer?"

"Everyone is a suspect until they're cleared."

"This is preposterous," Hall barked. "Just because CIRP had a little bad publicity doesn't mean that everyone here is a mad scientist or a criminal."

"I'm well aware of that." Mark maintained a level voice. "After all, you hired Claire Kos."

"She's only one of the many fine doctors we have on staff. But then again, you obviously have something personal going on with her."

"I knew Claire before."

"Before?"

"Yes, before the accident." He hesitated. "Did you?"

Hall shook his head. "No, I wish I had. She came here for rehab therapy. The therapist who worked with her bragged about her strength and courage, and when I found out she was a psychologist, I offered her a job."

"Because you were attracted to her?" Mark asked.

Hall's gaze turned cutting. "I don't like the implication."

"Exactly when did Claire come here?"

Hall crossed his arms. "About a year ago."

"Do you know the date of her accident?"

"You should ask Dr. Kos these questions. I hardly see how they're relevant to the case."

Mark fought his reaction. "I was just curious about her condition. Do you know if her eyesight can be restored?"

"I don't discuss my employees' personal or medical history with anyone, Agent Steele." He steepled his hands. "And to some people, her condition wouldn't matter."

Mark swallowed hard. Is that what Hall thought? And Claire? That he couldn't care for her because she was impaired? "Look, Hall, I simply want to help Claire, that's all."

"Then do your job and let her move on with her life."

Hall turned to his computer, firmly dismissing him. Mark bristled as the director shut the door behind him. Hall was the second person today to warn him away from Claire.

Did Hall simply want her for himself, or had Claire somehow indicated to him that she'd be happier without Mark?

Irked, he slipped out the door of the outer office, but he noticed the secretary wasn't at her desk. She'd obviously taken a break or was on an errand, so he borrowed her computer, then clicked several keys, searching for personnel and patient files. When he located Claire's file, he noted the day she'd arrived for therapy, her date of employment, then found a code that linked to her patient file. A second later, he skimmed the report.

Claire Kos had sustained a blow to her head in a serious automobile accident. When she regained consciousness, she'd lost her sight. Suddenly he heard footsteps approaching. Hall's secretary was returning. He didn't have time to read the rest of the file. But his stomach clenched when he saw the date of Claire's accident. The report also indicated it might be possible that she regain her sight. So why hadn't she?

The date flashed back again. Claire's accident occurred the very day he'd left for his mission. And she hadn't been too far from the airport.

Had she been coming to see him after all? If so, why hadn't she contacted him afterward?

AN IMAGE OF her scarf choking another woman played on Claire's mind. If the killer was someone she knew, she had to figure out who and why he was committing these crimes.

Her patient caseload was the most likely place to look. Joel Sanger? Richard Wheaton?

Wheaton entered her office, this time shrouded by a dark mood, his footsteps heavier than normal. Perhaps his adolescent side was emerging and trying to take dominance.

The teenager had protected the child Richard by destroying the cause of his abuse—his mother. Was he now transferring those feelings to other women and killing them?

"Richard?"

"It's Richie."

"Richie, have a seat and tell me what's going on."

"Don't feel like sittin'." He crossed the room in front of her, then stopped at the window, drumming his knuckles on the glass. "Life sucks."

"Why is that, Richie?"

"'Cause that social worker keeps bugging us."

"The social worker?" Claire mentally recalled the details from his file. When he was thirteen and his mother had died, the police had speculated that the woman's death was a suicide, but there had been no suicide note, so they'd written her death up as an overdose. Apparently heroin addicts didn't exactly garner sympathy or priority from police.

A social worker had attempted to place Richie in a foster home, but no one wanted the teenage son of an addict, so he'd been placed in a group home. From there, his history grew even shadier.

"You don't like Ms. Gridley?"

"Hell, no, she wants to split us up, stick us in some hole."

"Us?"

Silence met her question.

"How many of you are there?"

"We don't need anyone else. We take care of each other."

Claire's fingers tightened around her pen. "You take care of little Richie, don't you?"

He grunted. "Yeah, and that crybaby, Regina."

"Regina?"

He cursed again. "I shouldn't have told you about her, but she's a pain in the butt. Cries all the time. Makes Mama crazy mad."

"Can I meet Regina, Richie?"

Richie's shoes clicked on the floor as he walked toward her, then he sat down on the sofa. Seconds later, she heard a small childlike whine, then a tiny feminine voice.

"Tell me your name, sweetie," Claire said.

"R...egina."

"Hi, Regina. I'm Claire."

She heard a sucking sound and realized he was sucking his thumb. Earlier she'd spoken to the five-year-old little boy who'd witnessed his father die at the hands of his mother. Where had Regina been?

"How old are you, Regina?"

"Free."

"Three?"

"Uh-huh."

"Tell me about your mother, sweetie."

The sucking grew louder, then she started to cry. "She says I'm a bad girl, but I'm not."

Claire clenched her notepad. "No?"

"N...o, but she don't believe me." Her sobs grew louder. "She says she gots to punish me...."

"Regina, were you there when your father died?"

She whimpered. "No, I hidded in the cwoset, so she couldn't get me. Richie, he 'tects me."

"Why did your mother want to get you?"

A big sniffle escaped her. "'Cause I'm bad, I'm always bad—"

Suddenly Richie's voice broke in. "She can't talk anymore."

"Why not?" Claire reached out to comfort the child, but Richie pulled away, then stood and stomped back to the window.

"'Cause she went away."

Claire froze. The little girl had become one of Richard's alternate personalities? But had there been a real sister who had died?

Maybe, because she was a bad girl.

Chapter Eleven

Mark's chest was so tight he could barely breathe. The realization that Claire might have been on her way to see him the day he left for his mission changed everything.

While all the other soldiers had enjoyed a send-off with family surrounding them, their lovers and wives and children waving with tear-filled eyes, he'd stood to the side, waiting, praying, hoping Claire would arrive. He'd wanted to know that she would wait for him, but when she hadn't shown, he'd taken it as a clear sign that she didn't love him, that she'd declined his marriage proposal.

And then later she'd returned his ring via mail with a one-sentence typed declaration that she didn't want to marry him. It had been the only piece of mail he'd received while he was overseas. The cold gesture had hardened his heart and ripped his soul in two.

But if she'd had the accident on the way to the airport, had she been coming to say goodbye or to accept his proposal?

His heart pounded as he stalked from Hall's office toward the psychiatric wing. He had to know, and Claire would tell him the truth. She'd tell him every detail about that day, about her accident and her condition, and whether she really had loved him.

Another realization hit him—had Claire sent him that goodbye note because she was blind? Had she been afraid he couldn't accept her disability?

That would certainly account for her sister's attitude toward him. But hadn't Claire loved him enough to trust him?

The hurt added to the sinking premonition that he should have at least tried to contact her. He should have forced a confrontation instead of accepting her dismissal so readily. He'd just assumed she was like his mother.

He wouldn't accept a brush-off this time.

Determination made his stride brisk. He had fought a battle overseas for his country, now if he had to fight one at home to make her see that he loved her, he would. And he did love her.

He had never stopped loving her, even when he thought she'd refused to be his bride.

A renewed sense of calm washed over him as he entered her office. He smiled at her secretary. "I'm back to see Claire."

"I believe her appointment is just leaving."

He nodded and took a seat. Ten minutes later, a young man he guessed was in his early twenties walked out wearing a black leather jacket, black jeans and sunglasses. He ducked his head as he walked past, and

Mark watched, wondering at his story. Claire's secretary rose and knocked, then gestured for him to enter.

"Claire?" Although it had only been a couple of hours since he'd seen her, he was hungry for the sight of her. She'd pulled her loose curls back into a ribbon at the nape of her neck with a few loose tendrils dangling around her heart-shaped face, making her look young and delicate. His gaze dropped to the pale blue suit she wore and he had to smile. No suit could camouflage those feminine curves or hide the sensual woman beneath.

"Is something wrong, Mark?" She folded her hands and met him on the front side of her desk. "Do you have new information?"

"Yes, and no."

"What is it? Have the police found the killer?"

"No, not yet."

She sighed in disappointment.

"Why didn't you tell me you had your car accident the day I left to go overseas?"

Her sharp intake of breath indicated he'd caught her off guard. Good. The truth had certainly shaken him.

"I didn't think it mattered."

"Of course it mattered, especially if you were driving to the airport."

She bit down on her lip and started to turn away, but he caught her, held her arms in his grip. "You were coming to the airport, weren't you?"

Her breath quivered out.

"Tell me, Claire. For God's sake, I left that day believing you didn't love me, that you didn't care enough to even see me off to war."

"No…" her voice broke. "Mark, don't. Let it go."

"I can't let it go." He shook her gently. "You owe me the truth. I put my heart on the line, offered to share my life with you, and I got a damn note in the mail that was typed, not even handwritten. Do you have any idea how that made me feel?"

She dropped her head forward as if to look at her hands. "I couldn't see to write," Claire said, a trace of bitterness edging into her voice.

"What did the doctors say about your sight loss? Can you have surgery? A corneal transplant?"

She shook her head. It broke his heart. She had faced a major crisis all alone, had suffered without anyone to help her through the ordeal except her sister. Another reason Paulette hated him. Now that he knew the truth, he couldn't blame her.

"So, that's the reason you didn't contact me? You thought I wouldn't love you or want you because you're blind?"

She shook her head, tears brimming over her eyes. "Mark…"

"Tell me the truth, dammit."

"Yes," she whispered. "You deserved better."

He tried to calm his raging anger. On some level, he wondered what he would have done had he been in her shoes. On the other hand, she should have trusted him.

"But the report said you might regain your sight."

"The report was wrong," Claire said. "As you can see, my vision hasn't returned."

"Claire—"

"How did you find out about my accident?"

He hesitated, and her mood seemed to shift as she realized the obvious. "You read my medical files?" Anger tightened her mouth. "You had no right to pry into my personal life!"

"I wouldn't have if you'd told me yourself. But there's a chance you can see again. We'll do whatever it takes to make that happen."

"There is no *we,* Mark. And I'm perfectly satisfied with my life now. Except for this killer, I'm happy…"

He didn't believe her. Or maybe he was simply disappointed. He wanted her to want him. To want to see again. Didn't she want either? What had happened to the fighter in her?

"You won't even try?"

"I…I've adjusted to my life. There's no need."

His breath sounded harsh in the silence that followed. "Tell me this, Claire. What had you planned to tell me that day at the airport? Were you going to wear my ring and be my wife?"

She squeezed her fingers together. "Please, don't, Mark—"

"Tell me the truth. Were you going to say yes or no to my proposal?"

"Yes," she said in a haunted voice. "I wanted to be your wife. But it's too late for us now. We can't go back."

He'd thought she'd hurt him before, but other than losing his fellow soldiers that day, the pain that knifed through him now was sharper than anything he'd ever felt.

"What kind of man do you think I am?" He released

her, then stood back and stared at her. "I can't believe you intended to marry me, then decided your condition would make a difference so you didn't even send me word you were hurt. You really thought that little of me?"

He started toward the door. "Never mind. You already answered that question."

CLAIRE SAGGED into her office chair, drained from her encounter with Mark. The last thing she'd wanted to do was hurt him, but she obviously had. A year ago, when she hadn't shown up at the airport, and then today.

But he'd still had no right to snoop into her personal files.

And what did she really have to offer him? She could never be the perfect wife…

She covered her hands with her face. Why had she been driving during that storm? Even though that car had flown up on her tail, its lights blinding her, she should have started for the airport earlier. She should have called Mark and informed him she was on her way, so she wouldn't have felt the need to rush.

All the could-have-beens taunted her. The life they could have had if she hadn't crashed and lost their child. The homecoming she might have given him when he'd returned from fighting. The baby she would have held in her arms and presented to its father.

An aching emptiness settled in her as Mark's last hurt-filled accusations echoed in her ears. *What kind of man do you think I am, Claire? You really thought that little of me?*

"No, Mark," Claire whispered. "I love you too much to saddle you with my weakness." Worse, when he'd asked if her sight would return, she'd heard the hope in his voice. She couldn't live with that hope, not and disappoint him.

Because, in truth, she had no idea why her vision hadn't returned. She wasn't a candidate for a corneal transplant. In fact, the doctors had predicted that her eyesight would return on its own, that once the tissue healed and the swelling went down, she would see again. But so far, she hadn't, and she'd learned to deal with it.

Because your condition is psychosomatic.

She hated the word and what it implied, but deep down she feared it was true. She was causing her own blindness. What kind of woman did that make her? A shrink who couldn't heal herself....

Mark deserved a whole woman, one who could give him the happiness and love and passion he needed. She was just an empty shell running on autopilot, using her days to help others and trying not to dwell on the mistakes of her past.

A knock sounded and her secretary opened the door slightly. "Dr. Kos, Joel Sanger's probation officer just phoned. He's in lockup at county."

"What are the charges?"

"Drunk and disorderly. Seems he got mad at a waitress, lost his cool and created a scene."

Claire nodded. "All right, thanks." She checked her appointment calendar. She had a good two hours before her next patient. "Lindy, will you please call me a driver? I'm going to visit him at the jail." She didn't want to ask Mark to take her or ask questions about Sanger.

"Are you sure you want to do that, Dr. Kos?"

Claire nodded. "Yes. I'm his only hope. Maybe visiting him will tell me more about his condition." And maybe she'd be able to discern if he was responsible for killing the other women.

Then again, Richard Wheaton's visit had disturbed her. The personality of the little girl that had emerged had struck a chord of sympathy and familiarity within her. Regina's mother had called her a bad girl, then ended up dead. Claire believed Richard was responsible.

Wheaton fit the profile of a serial killer.

She massaged her temple, a headache pounding. She hated to admit it, but she might have to talk to the police. Richard was beginning to look more and more like the Midnight Murderer.

Could she find a way to have Mark check him out without compromising her ethical obligations to her patient and endangering Wheaton's treatment?

WHEN CLAIRE arrived at the jail, the officer in charge informed her Sanger was out of control. Bracing herself, she asked to be escorted to the cell where he'd been placed, determined to see if she could pry information from him.

The minute she made it to the cell, she heard footsteps pacing the cement floor like a caged animal.

"He's been flinging his arms and pacing like a madman for over an hour," the guard said.

Sanger screamed a string of obscenities and a non-sensical jumble of words.

"Mr. Sanger, it's Dr. Kos."

He either ignored her or didn't hear her, his rantings growing louder. "The angel comes, but he can't save me! The big red light, it's crashing on the earth now. There's fire."

"He's on the floor now," the guard said, "covering his head with his hands like he really believes that garbage. He also has a weird rash on his arms."

A rash? Claire remembered the ointment she'd smelled and wondered if Sanger had used it. She hadn't detected it on him during her sessions, but thought she did now.

"Hide, get away from it. It's exploding!" Sanger shouted. "We're all going to die!"

"Joel," Claire said softly. "It's Claire. You're safe now. There is no explosion." She paused, hoping she could break through, but he emitted a wailing, almost animal-like sound. "Look up at me, Joel. I'm here now, it's all right."

"No, you can't get me. Go away or I'll shoot!"

"He's a nutcase," the guard muttered.

Claire frowned. "He's suffering from a psychotic breakdown. He must have stopped taking his medication." She turned back to Sanger. "I'll be back, Joel. I'm going to get permission to move you to the psychiatric center for treatment." And she'd get them to check out the rash.

She allowed the guard to lead her back to the front office so she could follow through on her promise.

Had his mental instability triggered his violent tendencies to the point of murdering innocent women?

MARK PUT HIS EMOTIONS on hold as he drove back to the center. After he'd left Claire's office, he'd driven to the police station to see if the locals had any new information on the case. Along with Claire's help, the police had issued a general profile of the killer, but it was still vague, the factors that connected the victims even more so.

So far, each of the potential suspects, the relatives, boyfriends and husbands of the victims had been cleared. The nationwide database search hadn't offered any viable possibilities, either. They had discovered one case of a killer who fit the profile. He'd strangled three women in Las Vegas five years ago, but he was still serving time.

Except for Claire, they still hadn't discovered any connection between the victims. The M.E.'s report stated that each of the women had been injected with Percoset which had slowed her abilities prior to death, the reason there had been no visible signs of struggle. So far, none of the hospitals or other medical facilities had reported any significant quantities of the drug missing.

Lassiter, Ferguson and Hall all had easy access to pharmaceuticals at the center. Any one of them could have obtained what they'd need, although Hall's party had given them alibis for the latest murder. He personally disliked Lassiter and would like to see him charged, but they didn't have enough evidence to even bring him in.

The M.E. had pinpointed the odor Claire recognized as a new ointment similar to calamine lotion which was used to treat poison ivy, insect bites and other rashes. Scientists at CIRP had patented the cream and it was sold over the counter. Black and Fox were checking into that angle, but again, with tourist and mosquito season well underway, it would be virtually impossible to track down every person who'd purchased the ointment.

Mark couldn't rule out Claire's patients, either. Half of them were taking narcotics. They could have stolen a key to a pharmaceutical cabinet, talked an orderly into giving them extra drugs or obtained them on the streets.

Claire wouldn't like his questioning them, but she couldn't keep quiet and let another woman die.

He checked his watch, determined to arrive back at the center before Claire had to leave for the show. He didn't want her going anywhere alone.

A few minutes later he strode into her office, spoke to her secretary and claimed a seat. He thought through the details of the case while he waited, hoping to detect some link they hadn't noticed before but nothing registered. He phoned Devlin, but his co-worker confirmed that the case was at a standstill.

Frustration tightened Mark's shoulders as he realized another attack was imminent. The press had issued warnings again to all the single women in Savannah and the neighboring islands to avoid going out alone, and extra police had been brought in to stake out the beaches. But catching the guy in the act was a long shot. They needed definitive evidence.

The door opened, and Claire walked through the

doorway, her head lowered as she spoke to a young woman. The woman thanked her, then bypassed Mark without looking his way. It took a special sort of person to deal with the emotionally unstable patients Claire counseled.

"Claire, can we talk before we go to the station?"

She stiffened at the sound of his voice. "Sure, come in."

She walked back to her desk and took a seat, and he claimed the chair opposite her desk. "Mark, I'm sorry for this morning."

He knotted his hands, not ready to discuss their personal history yet. "We've pretty much reached a dead end with the suspect list. We need to look seriously at your patients."

She gripped the desk edge, then finally nodded. "I can't give you their files."

He had studied the problem on the way over, and they were still waiting on a court order. "All right, but let me see a list of male patients. I'll call out their names. If you think I should explore them, nod yes. If you don't feel they fit the profile, shake your head no."

Claire visibly relaxed. "I suppose that would be all right." A second later, she handed him a printout of her male patients. Only five fit the age range they believed to be the killer's.

"Chris Huet."

She shook her head no.

"Dan Buckner." No. "Randy Turst." No. "Joel Sanger."

She paused, then gave a clipped nod.

"Richard Wheaton?"

Another nod.

"All right, thanks for your cooperation."

"Is that it?"

"Yes, are you ready to go to the station?"

"Yes, let me get my things."

She reached for her purse and cane, and his heart squeezed again. This morning they'd seemed to be getting closer, but now the distance gaped even further between them, like a canyon he'd never be able to cross.

"GOOD EVENING, this is Dr. Claire Kos and you're listening to *Calling Claire*. Tonight we're going to talk about unconditional love." Claire paused. "Unconditional love means loving someone even though they're not perfect, even when they make mistakes. It also means sacrificing for the one you love. Perhaps those of you who have relationships where you feel you have unconditional love might want to share with us."

The first two callers relayed stories about sacrificing their own careers to put their husbands through school. "That is love," Claire said. "But don't forget, ladies, that in a relationship both people should sacrifice. If you've totally given up the things that are important to you, then you may resent that person later. You also may become someone different, someone less interesting than the person you once were. So don't sacrifice yourself. For a healthy relationship, both parties should be willing to compromise."

Maureen, a thirty-something stay-at-home mother, phoned in next. "I didn't understand unconditional love until I had children. But now, well, let's just say there's nothing my kids could do that would change my love for them."

Claire felt a pang of envy. "Most mothers feel that way," she said, although her own hadn't, and neither had the parents of some of her patients. "You can teach your child about that kind of love by being a role model, and by reassuring them that even when they disappoint you, and they will disappoint you at times, you still love them."

"You're right. I learned that from my own mother. I'm going to call her right now and thank her."

A few more women phoned in to talk about their unconditional love for their children, each one reminding Claire of her unborn baby. Sometimes she wondered if she would have had a boy or a girl, and if her child would have had Mark's striking dark hair and eyes or her own fair coloring.

The buzzer signal dinged again, and she answered the line, her nerves beginning to fray the closer it drew to midnight. "Hello, this is Claire."

"Claire," a male voice said in a muffled tone. "Your mother didn't love you that way, did she? She thought you were a bad girl."

Claire froze, then motioned for Mark and Bailey to make certain they switched the call to a private line, and that they recorded and traced the call.

"How do you know what my mother said to me?" Claire asked.

"Because you told me, Claire," he whispered. "I know *all* your secrets."

Her heart pounded. What did he mean, she had told him? She never talked about her past...except right after the accident. Even then, she'd seen a female doctor.

"I don't have secrets," Claire said, tensing even more at his bitter laugh.

"Oh, yes, you do, and I know them." His voice dropped to an eerie whisper. "I know why you lost your sight."

She sucked in a sharp breath. "Who is this?"

"But even blind, you see the good in people don't you, Claire?" he said, ignoring her. "In your patients, even if they're really, really bad."

"Yes, I believe everyone has good inside of them."

"Even if they're ugly on the outside?"

"Physical looks aren't important," Claire said. "And if you tell me where to meet you, I'll prove it to you."

Suddenly music piped in over the phone, the soft strains of a lullaby. Claire's heart clenched.

He knew her secrets. He knew why she couldn't see. Oh, God. He knew about the baby....

"Who is this?" she demanded. "Stop being a coward and tell me your name."

The phone went silent, the soft lullaby echoing in her mind.

Claire couldn't take any more. She had to get out of there. Take a break. Forget the grating sound of that sick man's voice.

She dropped the earphones and stumbled from the room.

"Claire, wait!" Mark called.

"No…I have to go to the ladies' room." She grabbed her cane and hurried down the hall, tears streaming down her face. Who could be doing this to her? And why taunt her with the memory of her lost child?

Feeling nauseous, Claire hurried into the bathroom, leaned over the sink, anguished sobs wracking her body. Footsteps clattered behind her. Someone had followed her inside the bathroom. "Mark?"

Heavy breathing echoed in reply.

Panic slammed into Claire. She swung her cane in front of her, and tried to run. But the man lunged forward, caught her and threw her up against the wall, then pressed a hand over her mouth, drowning out the sound of her cry. She batted at him with the cane, but he grabbed it and flung it across the room. The sound of it pinging off the wall reminded her of how helpless she'd become.

Seconds later, he dragged her out the door and into the stairwell. The scent of that medical cream made her dizzy, but she struggled anyway. Determined to escape, she brought her leg up and kicked backward, slamming into his kneecap.

He yelped and his legs buckled, but he tightened his grip on her. She screamed and they both went crashing down the stairs.

Chapter Twelve

The signal died just before Mark could trace it. He assumed it was another throwaway cell phone, and hoped the police staked out on the various beaches might pick up something.

His instincts on alert, he thanked Bailey, then strode down the hall to the ladies' room. He was worried about Claire. The stress and pressure were getting to her. She felt responsible for these other women which was totally unfair. She had her own demons to deal with.

He hadn't helped any by succumbing to his own hurt earlier and laying guilt at her feet. If she hadn't trusted him, then maybe she'd felt she had a reason.

Maybe he was to blame.

He knocked on the ladies' room door. "Claire?" No answer. He knocked again. "Claire, it's Mark. Are you all right?"

Again, no answer.

Fear slammed into him, and he knocked louder, then opened the door. "Claire, are you in here?" When she didn't reply, he stormed inside and checked the stalls. "Claire!" It was empty.

Then he saw her cane lying on the floor, and his heart nearly stopped.

He jerked himself out of his stupor and rushed outside, checked the station room to see if she had returned. Bailey shook his head, looking harried with the program and perplexed that Claire had run out.

"Alert security," Mark yelled as he ran down the hall. He spotted the stairwell door swinging, and peered inside, his gun drawn. "Claire?"

A muffled cry floated through the silence. "Claire?"

"Mark!"

He heard her voice, then footsteps running down the stairs. He jumped the steps two at a time. Hurtling around the landing, he raced down the next set, his heart in his throat. Claire was trying to stand up, holding on to the wall, her skirt and hair disheveled. She swung her arms in an arc to orient herself. He launched over the last step and helped her stand.

"Mark," she said in a choked voice. "He was here. He grabbed me!"

Mark's heart leapt to his throat. He searched the stairwell but saw nothing. Rage flew through him as he dragged Claire into his arms and held her tight.

What would he do if he lost her again?

THE NEXT HOUR passed in a blur for Claire as Mark hustled her to the station room and checked with security. Detective Black and the local law enforcement had arrived on the scene in minutes, combing the surrounding area. But the station was set in downtown Savannah. If the killer had snuck out, he could have slipped into the crowd of summer tourists and any number of restaurants or bars unnoticed.

The security guards hadn't caught anyone entering or exiting. Mark ordered them to recheck the tapes, although he was afraid it was fruitless. He didn't know how the killer was getting into the building without being detected, but he had—twice.

Drew ran in, frantic. "My God, Claire, are you all right?"

She nodded, still shaken.

"Where were you?" Mark asked.

"Downstairs preparing for the morning show," Drew said.

"Can anyone vouch for your whereabouts?" Mark asked.

Claire tensed.

"I can't believe this!" Drew's voice rose in anger. "You think I'd hurt Claire?"

"I have to account for everyone in the building," Mark said. "And the last time Claire received a call, you weren't upstairs with her."

Claire frowned and pulled at Mark's hand. "Mark—"

"I'm just doing my job," Mark barked. "Can anyone account for you?"

"The coproducer," Drew said. "Check with him yourself."

Mark phoned downstairs. Just as Drew said, the coproducer verified his story. Drew was not the killer.

Mark clutched Claire's hand. "Come on, I'm taking you home."

Claire couldn't help herself. She clung to Mark, hating the darkness. Yet, she was trapped there with the memories. And now the voices of the dying women crying for help, the voice of the killer whispering that they were bad girls.

The voice of the man who knew her secrets.

Secrets she had yet to share with Mark.

A security guard spoke in a clear tone, "We'll review the tapes again and see if we can come up with anything. But so far, there's nothing suspicious."

"Call me on my cell if you do." Mark pulled Claire to a standing position. "Let's go." She didn't argue. It was already past one o'clock and she was exhausted.

Had the killer left her and gone in search of another victim?

She shivered and Mark wrapped an arm around her, cradling her close as they walked to the car. Their earlier interlude was forgotten, although tension of another kind brewed between them.

Claire had almost been abducted by the killer. She could have died....

Mark stroked her hand over and over as he drove, his breathing unsteady. She clung to his fingers, grateful to have the human contact. She didn't want to be alone tonight.

She didn't want Mark to leave her.

The sounds of traffic and the radio calmed her slightly, then Mark parked and she tensed again. "You don't think he came here, do you?"

"No, he took enough chances tonight. He's probably holed up some place waiting for the police to disperse." She reached for the car door and he gripped her hand. "But I'll check the cottage first. Wait here and lock the door."

Claire clutched his hand. "No…please let me go with you."

"Claire—"

"I don't want to be alone."

A long silence stretched between them. She wondered if Mark realized her comment was an invitation. He had no idea how much that cost her.

"I don't plan to leave you alone," he said in a gruff voice.

The car door squeaked open, and he came around for her. She grabbed her cane, but allowed him to take her hand this time, and they walked up the sidewalk together. He found himself silently counting the steps, acclimating to the way Claire walked. When they reached the cottage, she handed him her key and let him unlock the door. He led her inside slowly, careful to keep her behind him. She sensed that he'd drawn his gun and felt marginally better knowing Mark was there to protect her.

Five minutes later, he'd searched the entire house and found it empty. A few minutes later, Mark spotted a bottle of merlot she had in the kitchen and poured her a glass. "Here, drink this. It might help you relax."

She didn't argue. She swirled the liquid in the glass, then took a sip and savored the tart taste. "Are you having one?"

"I don't want wine," Mark said.

"I'm sorry, I don't have anything stronger—"

"I don't want alcohol at all," he said in a gruff voice. "I want you, Claire."

Claire's breath rushed upward, then got trapped in her chest.

Without another word, he took the glass from her, then dragged her into his arms and kissed her.

NO SOONER had Mark touched Claire than he felt his control slipping. Once he'd thought he'd loved her, but nothing compared to the emotions he felt at the moment.

She had almost been kidnapped by a madman tonight. A madman who was killing innocent women, one who'd chosen Claire as the target of his demented games.

A man who might have killed her or done God knew what, had she not fought back.

He teased her lips apart with his tongue and explored her mouth, driven by need and the desire to feel her come alive in his arms. He desperately wanted to erase the darkness she lived in, but he couldn't.

He could make her forget the horrifying memory of her earlier attack though, if just for a little while. And he could chase away his own demons with the feel of her lush body against his and bury the pain of losing her by easing himself inside her once again.

Heat blazed between them as he walked her back to her bedroom. Then he undressed her, tossed her skirt to the floor, and stared at her soft, delicate bare skin in the moonlight. Her curves taunted him, her scent intoxicated him, and his sex surged, begging for release.

"Mark?" Her voice sounded suddenly shy, unsure, and he realized he had the advantage. She could no longer look at his body, see the desire and hunger in his eyes.

"You are so beautiful," he whispered in a guttural tone. "My God, Claire, I couldn't stand to lose you again."

She wet her lips and his legs nearly buckled.

Then she reached out a slender hand, inviting him to her bed. He accepted it, feeling almost reverent.

Lowering her to the duvet, he cradled the back of her neck, and tasted the salty sweetness of her skin, then nibbled at the sensitive shell of her ear, then lower, to lick along her breasts. The soft mounds bulged over the lace bra she wore, but he left it in place, first teasing and suckling her through the flimsy barrier until she bucked and threaded her hands in his hair. He brought the tips to hard points, driving them both insane, and finally, unveiled them to lick her bare skin.

"Mark, you feel so good."

"I love the way you taste," he whispered in the darkness. "In the desert, I used to wake up hard, dreaming about you."

He suckled her harder, lifting and kneading her breasts until she moved her leg in between his.

She raked his back with her hands then pushed him to his knees. "Take off your clothes," Claire murmured. "I want to feel you, touch you, hold you."

He did as she asked, tossing his shirt and jeans to the

floor. Claire rose to her knees, her rose-tipped breasts swaying gently as she slid her hands to his face. He froze, the air trapped in his lungs as she touched his jaw. He wondered what she was thinking, if she still remembered what he looked like.

She ran her fingers over his eyes, across his cheeks, then along his jawbone. "You always had such strong cheekbones," she whispered. "So commanding. Powerful."

His lips parted in a deep breath as she gently caressed his face. She was seeing him through her touch, he realized, memorizing the details. He'd never imagined how erotic it might be to rely on his other sensations, but without sight, her sense of touch and smell must be heightened.

Then her fingers danced across his chest. Brushed his nipples. Tangled in the coarse hair on his chest. He hardened, his control on the edge of shattering. Nothing had ever felt so titillating.

Her fingers trailed lower, inched into the waistband of his boxers, and she began to slide them down his hips. He watched her, saw rapture and seduction plainly written on her face, the faint wicked smile lighting her mouth spiking his fever even more. Her fingernails teased the firm muscles rippling in his thighs as he raised his hips. Then he was naked. Claire reached for his sex, cupped it in her hand and began to stroke him.

"Claire…"

"I dreamt about doing this," she groaned. "And this." She licked at his skin, then lower to his nipples, suckling him as he had done to her.

He nearly exploded, groaning in pleasure-pain.

She smiled into his chest, then tried to shift lower, teasing his belly.

"No, not yet. It's been too long, and I'm too close."

Holding his raging need for release at bay, he kissed her again and stroked her skin, her hips, then lower where he eased her legs apart. She shifted into his hand, and he pushed her legs wide, then slid his fingers into her slick moistness. His lips found a path down to her breasts again, and he teased her nipples, his heart pounding when she trembled beneath him. She was tight, sweet, moist, waiting for him to fill her.

He eased her to her back, making her wait longer.

"Please, Mark."

"First, I have to taste you." She gripped his shoulders to stop him, but he was desperate to have his way. His body quivered from the fire spreading through his veins as he kissed her belly, then trailed hot, wet kisses lower to her inner thighs, before dipping his tongue inside her.

She bucked upward instantly, but he pushed her legs further apart and tasted, exploring, sating his hunger for her at last.

"Please, I need you now."

This was the Claire he knew. She asked for the things she needed, she gave but she took from him as well. "I need you, too." He rose and looked at her face, his heart squeezing. He wanted her to open her eyes, look into his and see how much he wanted her. The thought that she couldn't see him nearly broke his heart.

He'd have to make it up to her with his touch.

"Hold on, baby." Shifting above her, he cupped her hips, lifted them upward and eased his length inside her. He was aching, and only she could offer him what he needed. He filled her, pushing inside slowly so she could adjust to his size, then moved deeper and deeper, groaning with satisfaction. He had finally come home.

CLAIRE ARCHED her back, throwing every ounce of her being into their lovemaking. As much as she wanted to see Mark's face, her other senses were on overload. The scent of his skin was exhilarating. Sensations rippled through her as she ran her hands over his body. She memorized the hard planes and angles, the coarse hair on his chest and legs, the scrape of his beard stubble against her.

She reveled in the moans that erupted from his throat, in the hungry way he possessed her, in the gentle way he slid his finger between her lips so she could taste herself. She sucked his fingers one by one, her body quaking as he slid the tip in and out of her mouth. She raked her fingers down his back and over the steely muscles of his hips, then wrapped her legs around his waist, smiling when he clenched in response.

Mark's lovemaking was primal as he thrust inside her, harder and faster. She held on, clinging to the edge of control, afraid to jump off the ledge without him, but the power in his touch tore down her defenses, and she felt herself slipping over the edge.

"Come for me, Claire," he whispered on a throaty moan.

He withdrew slightly, leaving her begging for him to fill her again, then he stroked her with his erection, tormenting her until she could stand it no longer.

She flipped him to his back, straddled him, then lowered herself on his hard length, throwing back her head and body in wild abandon as she ran her hands over his chest. He was thick and hard and made her whole again.

Márk gripped her hips, supporting her, his lips finding her breasts and suckling her again, the erotic sound sending pinpoints of pleasure through her. She quivered, crying out his name as the sheer bliss of being with him again carried her through the storm. Mark met her explosive climax with a final grinding of his hips that triggered his own release, the two of them floating to the stars together.

In the aftermath, Mark rolled Claire to his side, cradled her in his arms and dropped soft kisses into her hair. Claire closed her eyes, not wanting anything to intrude on the moment. For the past year, she had lived in a vast, endless sea of darkness.

Mark had given her a sweet moment of light.

She held on to that euphoria, allowing his touches and kisses to soothe away the horror of the past, and the reason Mark had come back to her. As if he could read her mind, they made love again, slowly, sweetly, tenderly.

Finally sated, they fell into an exhausted sleep, lying spoon style together as they shut out the reality of their world.

But still, Claire couldn't promise Mark that she would ever see again.

Worse, she still bore her shameful secret.

Their time together couldn't last forever, but she would cling to it for just a little longer.

HE FLEXED his hands and gritted his teeth, willing himself to stop shaking, but pure frustration and rage trembled through him. Claire was in bed with Mark Steele.

She had been a bad girl.

He was so disappointed that tears filled his eyes and trickled down his unshaven jaw. He swiped them away with his sleeve, then clawed at the red welts on his arms, willing those away, too.

At least Claire wouldn't be able to see them. She would only see the good inside him, just as she did her lunatic patients.

Claire was supposed to be his. She had said goodbye to Mark a year ago. So why had she allowed him back in her life?

Because he didn't know her secrets. And she wanted to keep it that way.

Yes, Claire was a naughty girl, keeping things from him.

He unpocketed his cell phone, punched in her home number, and exhaled to steady his breathing. He refused to act nervous. No. He would stand his ground and fight for Claire like a man.

The phone rang three times before she answered. "Hello."

He closed his eyes at the sound of her sultry voice. "Hello, Claire." He hesitated, knowing she was sitting up now, realizing he'd gotten braver by calling her home.

"Claire, he doesn't really love you, not like I do."

"Who is this?"

"Have you told him about the miscarriage?"

Her breathing grew ragged. "Tell me who you are."

"I can give you another baby, Claire. We can replace the child you lost with one of our own."

He smiled at himself, then froze when the phone clicked into silence.

How dare she hang up on him!

Had Steele been listening?

A smile creased his lips at the thought. It would only be a matter of time before things fell apart again for Claire. And he would be there to pick up the pieces.

Just as he had the time before.

She still had no idea that both times he'd set the wheels in motion to bring her to him.

And this time, when he finally had her, they would be together forever.

Chapter Thirteen

Claire dropped the phone, choking on her own indrawn breath. How could the killer know about her baby? Other than her sister and the hospital staff who'd treated her after the accident, she had told no one. Except...

"Claire?"

Mark had heard the conversation. The minute the phone had rung, she'd indicated it was the killer, and he'd picked up the extension in the den. He stood at the doorway, his silence deafening.

She pulled the sheets up to cover herself, hating the fact that he could see her naked and vulnerable when she couldn't look into his eyes and read his thoughts.

Then again, maybe it was better she couldn't see, or she'd have to face the condemnation in his eyes. And she should have kept the caller on the line for the trace—

"Did you get his location?"

"No." His voice rushed out in a haunted whisper. "What did he mean about the baby?"

"I don't know," she said in a hoarse voice.

"Don't lie to me, Claire." He strode toward her and dropped down onto the bed. Claire shifted against the pillows to escape, but he gripped her arms. "What was he talking about? Did you have a baby?"

Claire shook her head, tears blurring her eyes and sliding down her cheeks. "No."

"Were you pregnant?"

The time for reckoning had come. She could hide no longer. She closed her eyes and nodded, a sob escaping her.

His fingers tightened almost painfully around her arms. "Was it mine?"

Pain clawed at her throat and chest. "Yes. Of course it was yours."

"Why didn't you tell me?"

"Because you were gone," Claire cried.

"What happened?"

She closed her eyes, seeing the bloody water all over again. He seemed to realize he was holding her too tightly and dropped his hands. Silence stretched tautly between them. A bird twittered outside, the wind brushed a branch against the windowpane.

Claire heard her own heart pounding in her chest.

"Tell me what happened, dammit."

She reached for her robe, dragged it on, tightened the belt. She was so cold. "I had a miscarriage," she cried. "I was going to tell you about the baby…at the airport that day you were leaving…"

"But you never made it to the airport because of the accident?"

She nodded, memories flooding her. "I was so excited," she whispered, then gestured toward the heart-shaped frame on her nightstand. "I bought that little picture frame. I was going to give it to you, and put the first picture of our baby in it." Her voice broke off.

"You lost our baby in the accident?"

She nodded again, then wrapped her arms around herself, trying to hold herself together, but the pain was too much. She doubled over and released an anguished cry.

ANGER, SHOCK, HURT, all bombarded Mark, robbing the air from his lungs. While he'd flown off to save the country thinking Claire hadn't loved him, she'd been on her way to accept his proposal and tell him that he was going to be a father—only she'd had a car accident. Worse, she'd lost their child.

Then she'd woken up sightless and alone.

He should have been there to save her and their baby. Or at least to comfort Claire afterward, to help her through the recovery process.

The guilt of losing his men and now his child felt like a crushing weight on him. He had no idea how to rectify the past. And he certainly didn't deserve a future with Claire, not after he'd let her down.

But he couldn't stand to see her in pain.

He tentatively reached out to hold her, but she curled away into a ball on the bed. A sharp stabbing pain tore through him at her withdrawal. No wonder Claire had been so distant when he'd first arrived.

She blamed him for deserting her.

If he hadn't been leaving that day, if he hadn't asked

her to come to the airport to send him off, she wouldn't have been driving in that storm. Then she wouldn't have had the accident.

And they might have had a baby.

He pictured a little girl or boy with Claire's blond curls and realized he'd lost the chance for that when he'd chosen his job over Claire. Now he understood why she'd run from him when he'd tried to get closer to her again.

And to think, he'd felt sorry for himself, that she hadn't come to the airport, that he had nobody to come home to, when he could have had a wife and child. Just like Abe…only Abe was gone, too….

Reeling with emotions, he went to the bed. He had to make her see how sorry he was.

"Claire…" he choked, then cleared his throat. "God, Claire, I'm so sorry…."

She tried to quiet her cries, and his heart ached. He crawled onto the bed beside her and curved an arm around her, pulling her to him spoon style. She stiffened, but he refused to release her. Instead, he tightened his arm around her and tried to absorb the tremors in her body. "I didn't know, Claire. If I had…if I had I would have come back. I would have found a way. You have to believe me." He pulled her closer, nuzzling her hair, guilt clawing at him. "I'm so sorry I let you down, that I wasn't there for you…for our baby…"

Claire's tortured breath rattled out. "I…wanted to call you," she whispered. "But then…then I couldn't…I couldn't talk about it."

He stroked her hair, his other hand slipping to her

stomach, but she stiffened again, and he moved it to her side.

"I know your job is important," she said, her tears subsiding slightly. "It's your life."

"You're important, too," he said, his emotions on the surface. "You have to know that, Claire. And I thought you understood why I had to go. I thought I was doing the right thing."

"I know." She swiped at her eyes, then turned to face him, the desolation in her eyes rocking him to the core. "And I thought I was doing the right thing by not calling you."

Because she couldn't forgive him?

He couldn't bring himself to ask the question. Instead, he slid his fingers along her hairline, itching to sink his fingers in the strands and bury his pain by sinking himself inside her.

But she obviously didn't want that. And she hadn't thought he could give her what she needed or she would have called him.

Claire slid from his embrace and sat up, turning to face the wall. "Please, Mark, go now. I need to be alone for a while."

Reeling with emotions, he swung his legs to the other side.

She stood, facing the wall, and his boots hit the floor with a thud. "For God's sake, talk to me." His voice rose, then he circled the bed to her, and gripped her arms, forcing her to face him. "Yell at me, scream at me, hit me if you want to. Hell, blame me, just don't shut me out again."

She shook her head, her voice so low he could barely hear it when she spoke. "Please go, Mark. I can't deal with this anymore."

She looked so fragile. And she was still so far away from him. "I don't want to leave you."

Her labored sigh drifted on the air between them. "But you're going to," she finally said.

"No, let's hash this out."

"I don't want to hash it out!" Claire knotted her hands into fists. "I'm tired, Mark. It's been a long day, a long month, hell, a long year. I just want to be alone. Can't you understand that?"

Emotions and indecision wound his stomach into a knot. Did she really hate him that much? If he forced her to talk, would he push her over the edge?

Her lip trembled, and even though she couldn't see it, he caught her turning in the direction of the small picture frame again. Caution won out.

"All right, but I'll be back." He leaned forward and gently brushed a kiss across her temple. "This isn't over, Claire. We will talk again."

She bit her lip but didn't reply. He hesitated at the doorway, drank in her beauty, then walked outside, cold and alone. An image of that empty picture frame flashed into his mind, and he scrubbed a hand over his face.

He hadn't realized he'd been crying until he felt the moisture on his fingertip. He wiped it away, then felt another fall in its place.

Dear God, how had everything become such a mess? How could he forgive himself for hurting her and their baby? And how could he make Claire love him again?

MARK HAD NO IDEA where he was going, but he had to take a drive. Knowing he couldn't leave Claire unprotected, he phoned Detective Black and waited nearby until he sent a squad car to watch Claire. Then he drove and drove and drove, hoping the hum of his engine would drown out the roar of his aching heart.

It didn't.

Finally, he glanced at the sign and realized he was in Brunswick, South Georgia.

The small town where Abe had lived.

He automatically reached inside his pocket, felt for the dog tags and knew why he'd ended up here.

He should have come sooner.

It took him ten minutes to find the small clapboard house that his friend had been so proud of. For a few seconds, he sat and simply stared at the yard. The small bicycle on its side. A swing set in the back with a tree fort. Abe had told him about building it with his boy.

Bone-tired and bracing himself for Marie's accusing eyes, he parked and walked up the sidewalk. The heat was sweltering, his shirt sticking to his chest, the cloying scent of his own fear surrounding him.

He had been a coward not to visit her.

Seeing Abe's face in his mind, he raised his hand and knocked on the door. He owed this to his buddy.

Seconds later, he heard footsteps and a small red-haired boy opened the door, his front teeth missing, a petite red-haired woman rushing up behind him.

"Kevin, I told you not to open the door to—" Her voice died as she saw him.

"Marie? I'm Lt. Mark—"

"Steele." She nodded. "I know who you are."

He swallowed hard, wondering if her son knew.

"Come in."

Her invitation surprised him. The boy was the spitting image of his father, only Abe hadn't been innocent, not after a few months in the war.

"I would have come sooner, but I was in the hospital, and then…" He let the sentence trail off, then realized he was being a coward again. "I didn't know what to say."

"I'm glad you're here, Mark." Marie's smile grew teary as she patted her son's head. "Kevin and I wanted to meet you, to talk to you."

She gestured toward the small plaid sofa and he stepped over some toys. Kevin sat down beside him, hands on his upraised knees and stared at him, his knees poking through the holes in his jeans. He wore an Atlanta Braves T-shirt. How many times had Abe talked about taking his son to his first game?

"Were you in the service with my father?"

Mark nodded, nearly choked. "Yes, he was my best friend."

"We missed you at the memorial service," Marie said in a low voice.

"Tell me about my dad," Kevin said, wide-eyed. "Was he a hero like they said?"

Mark didn't hesitate. "Yes, he definitely was a hero." Mark glanced at Marie's hopeful expression. It encouraged him, so he described how they'd met, how they sat around the fire at night and shared stories about their families, how proud Abe was of his son, how much he'd wanted to go to that Braves game with him. Kevin and Marie listened, tears sliding down Marie's cheeks occasionally, Kevin's eyes were red-rimmed as well, but also exhilarated by hearing details about his father.

Where were the accusations he had expected?

"He wrote us about you," Marie said. "And the other men in the platoon. You were all such good friends to him."

Mark nodded. "I have something for you," Mark finally said. He reached into his pocket and drew out the dog tags. They jangled as he handed them to Kevin. "Your father wanted you to have these."

Kevin's hand shook slightly as he accepted them, his face etched in awe as he slid the chain around his neck. Mark knew he had done right in coming to visit.

"You were with him when…at the end?" Marie asked in a thick voice, a voice desperate for any word from the man she'd loved.

He nodded, emotions clogging his throat as he looked down at Abe's son. "The last thing he said was to tell you both that he loved you." He rubbed Kevin's hair, silently vowing to make sure he saw that baseball game. "He was so proud of you, he couldn't wait to come home to you both."

Marie covered her mouth with a soft cry, and pulled Kevin to her. Then Kevin reached out to hug him. Mark dragged the boy into his arms and patted his back, taking Marie's hand in his as the three of them grieved for her husband.

"I'm so glad you were with him," Marie said quietly.

He nodded, wanting to apologize. "I wish I could have saved him."

She squeezed his hand. "You were there at the end, that's all that matters, that he wasn't alone."

"No," Mark said gruffly. "He wasn't alone. He had the two of you with him in his heart."

"And he always will," Marie whispered.

Kevin rubbed his father's dog tags in reply.

FINALLY, after making Marie and Kevin promise that if they needed anything, they'd call him, Mark composed himself enough to return to Claire's. He couldn't bring back their baby, but he could help Claire fight to get her life back.

Tension stretched between them as he entered the kitchen. He poured himself some coffee to occupy his hands and went straight to the point. "I'm sorry for leaving you like that."

"I understand."

Did she? He wasn't sure he did.

Then again, Claire had always been intuitive. But this wasn't about him or alleviating his guilt, it was about helping her. "Have you seen any specialists about your sight, Claire?"

She turned away from him. "I don't want to discuss it, Mark."

He gripped her arm. "Why not?"

"Because I've accepted my condition. Anyone who wants to be my friend has to accept me the way I am, too."

"We're hardly just friends, Claire."

He traced a finger over her chin. "And it's not that I can't accept your vision loss." He thought of Abe and his wife and son and all they had lost. How short life was. How they had to grab every moment and hang on. "But if there's a chance someone can help you, don't you want to try?"

"I told you, Mark, I'm fine now. I won't see any more doctors."

She darted into the shower, ending the discussion, and making Mark feel as if she'd cut him out of her life once again.

He heard the water running and stared at the rumpled covers in the bedroom, unable to believe that just last night and then again in the wee hours of the morning, he and Claire had been making love, forging a new bond that he'd hoped would last forever.

But too much had happened between them.

He wanted to tell her he could accept things the way they were. But if there was a chance she could see again, he wasn't sure he could accept her giving up. The Claire he'd known had been a fighter.

But he couldn't force her to love him. There was only one thing left to do now. Find the killer. Then let Claire get on with her life.

When she entered the kitchen, her hair was still damp, dangling in soft ringlets around her shoulders. She had dressed in another suit, a dark green one this time, that flattered her curves but looked professional.

In spite of the tension between them, his body reacted to the memory of those curves, naked and supple in his hands, and he hardened instantly, aching for her again.

"We need to talk," he said.

She nodded and walked to the coffeepot. He frowned at the sight of her trembling hands as she filled her cup. She looked exhausted, the strain of the morning and the caller wearing on her. Still, he was amazed at her strength and how self-sufficient she'd become without her sight. But simple tasks like pouring coffee took more concentration for her, another reminder of what she'd lost.

He wouldn't let the killer get to her again.

"Claire, who else did you tell about the miscarriage?"

A pained look tightened her mouth. "No one."

"No one?"

"Paulette."

"Who else?"

"Just the doctors and nurses who treated me after the accident."

"There has to be someone else." Mark sighed in frustration. "Or how else would the Midnight Murderer know you'd lost a child?"

"I'VE BEEN ASKING myself the same question over and over again." She sat down at the table and hugged her cup with her hands, hoping to warm herself. Although she desperately wanted to slide back into Mark's embrace, to turn back the clock to the night before when he'd lain entwined with her and she'd felt optimistic about their relationship, everything had changed. Now he knew the truth; about their child, about her vision impairment, about her imperfections.

He must blame her for their child's loss. And if she couldn't forgive herself, how could she expect him to?

"Did you tell Dr. Lassiter? Ian Hall? Dr. Ferguson?"

She shook her head no.

"What about your patients?"

"I never disclose personal information to a patient." She hesitated. "And as far as Joel Sanger, he was admitted to the psychiatric ward last night and is under heavy medication, so that rules him out."

"Could someone have hacked into your medical records?" he asked.

"I suppose it's possible."

Mark drummed his fingers on the table. "You seemed so sure about the doctors who treated you when you first had the accident. Maybe I should investigate—"

"But the doctor who treated me when I was admitted was female. When I came to CIRP for rehab therapy, my therapist was also female." A sudden memory broke through the haze of ones she'd tried to forget. "Although…"

"Although what, Claire?"

She pressed a hand to her mouth. She'd tried to block out most of those first few months after the accident. The pain had been so intense, one day had bled into another.

"What is it? Even the smallest detail might prove helpful."

"I went to a support group for a while," she said in a low voice.

A heavy sigh escaped him. Pity probably.

"It was led by a male doctor?"

"No. But there was a man in the group who tried to befriend me. I'd forgotten about him."

"Go on."

"I…I can't remember his name. I didn't think much of it at the time. I was too wrapped up in my own problems. But he asked me to go out for coffee a couple of times."

"What did you tell him?"

"I said no, Mark. I wasn't looking for another romance."

She chewed her bottom lip. "But that was so long ago. I doubt he'd bother me now. I haven't heard from him in months." She stood and paced to the window. "In fact, I don't even know where he is."

"Were all the members of the group suffering from vision problems?"

"No." Claire strained to remember the various situations. "There were four women, three men. One of the men was in his eighties, he'd recently lost his wife. Another was a teenager, he accidentally killed his best friend in a DUI related automobile accident."

"And the man who approached you?"

"He was probably in his early thirties." She hesitated, remembering how lonely he'd sounded. "An ex-military man. I believe he fought in Desert Storm. He was suffering from posttraumatic stress disorder." She hesitated, knowing Mark could relate.

"Think hard, Claire, do you remember his name?"

She shook her head. "I'm sorry, I didn't pay much attention to him. Then I dropped out of the group. I don't even know what happened to him."

"Can you get me a list of the people who attended?"

She nodded. "But Mark, I really don't think this guy is a killer."

"Maybe not, but we've hit dead ends so far. We have to check it out."

She set her coffee cup in the sink. "All right, then let's go. I have an appointment with a patient first thing." She refrained from telling him that her patient was Richard Wheaton. Wheaton had once worked for a computer company. If anyone could hack into her files, it would be him.

And he definitely fit the profile of the killer.

MEMORIES OF Mark's own stint in Desert Storm surfaced.

In the aftermath of a surprise bombing attack, he'd been trapped in the rubble of an explosion with three other guys. He'd finally been able to free himself, then help the others escape. Only one poor guy had begged to be left to die.

Mark shuddered at the memory. Apparently, the man thought he was going to be paralyzed, and had believed a life without legs wasn't worth living. He'd cursed Mark for setting him free, claiming he'd taken him from one hell to the next.

But Mark hadn't been able to leave a man to die.

But this case wasn't about him. The killer was someone who'd obviously become obsessed with Claire.

As soon as they arrived at her office, she phoned the counselor in charge of the support group and explained the circumstances, then handed Mark a list of the people who'd attended. Claire even balked at that, worried she was breaking doctor's privilege, but he agreed to use discretion. Only one name on the list was of interest, though. Al Hogan, the man who'd expressed interest in Claire.

Mark phoned Devlin and explained the most recent turn of events. "Listen, Devlin, I have two names I want you to run. Al Hogan and Richard Wheaton. Hogan was in a support group Claire attended and is a war vet. He was interested in Claire, but she refused his advances."

"Got it," Devlin said. "Who's the other man, Wheaton?"

"A patient of Claire's. Let me know what you find."

"I will. Where are you now?"

"On my way to talk to one of the women in the support group. I'm going to see if Hogan approached any of the other females, find out what their impressions of him were."

"Sounds like a plan. I'll get back to you as soon as possible."

Mark hung up, his nerves tight. The fact that the killer had attacked Claire, then phoned her at home proved he was taking chances. He was also growing more dangerous. Mark had to find him before he killed again.

Before he returned for Claire.

AT THE OFFICE, Claire learned Richard Wheaton had phoned in to reschedule his appointment, so she'd dropped by the psychiatric wing and visited Joel Sanger. Just as she'd expected, he had been medicated during the night and was still incoherent. Dr. Ferguson had ordered a complete battery of tests to eliminate the possibility of a brain tumor or some other physical reason for his condition. They were also testing the odd rash on his arms.

Then she checked with Dr. Ferguson and with the medical hospital in Atlanta to verify that her personal files and medical history hadn't been confiscated. Both places assured her that they had had no inquiries, although they couldn't be positive that someone hadn't hacked into the system. They did have special security codes to avoid such hacking, but an expert, especially someone with knowledge of medical software, might have found a way around the system.

Not a comforting thought.

Richard Wheaton had not only been a computer programmer, but he'd once worked for a large pharmaceutical company. He had knowledge of medical software and knew how to circumvent various security systems.

She should share this information with Mark, but she still felt uncomfortable disclosing details pertaining to her patients. If Wheaton wasn't the killer, then she would stir up problems for him that would ruin their professional relationship, problems which might set Wheaton back years in the recovery process.

She wouldn't be able to live with herself if that happened.

Yet, how could she let him kill again, if he was the killer?

The phone rang, and she was surprised to find her

Atlanta physician back on the line. "I know we just talked," he said, "but one of my nurses informed me that someone from the FBI had accessed your file. I don't know why they'd be interested, Claire, but I thought you should know."

Claire grew livid. Mark had been prying into her personal files again? Looking for information about her condition? He had no right…

And now, he most likely knew that the doctors believed her blindness to be psychosomatic. He must think she was crazy. Maybe he'd even made love to her out of sympathy, and some misguided hope of helping her regain her sight.

She hung up, but by the time Wheaton arrived her nerves were splintered. She had to finish this case and get Mark out of her life. She'd accepted her blindness, her limitations. She didn't need him making her question herself, or her sanity.

A knock sounded, and she jerked back to the present as her patient entered.

"Hello, Richard."

"Dr. Kos."

So, he was the adult man today. She never knew which personality to expect. But she needed to access Richie, the angry adolescent.

She inhaled, searching for the odor she related to the killer, but detected the faint scent of salt and sweat instead. "How are you feeling today?"

He settled onto the couch. "Tired."

"Did you have a rough night?"

"Yes." His voice sounded agitated.

"Is that the reason you rescheduled your appointment?"

"Yes." He hesitated and she waited patiently, silently encouraging him to offer more. "I woke up on the beach this morning. I…" his voice broke. "I can't remember how I got there."

She struggled not to react to that fact, knowing that all of the victims were found on the beach. "Do you go to the beach a lot?"

"Sometimes."

"You've had these blackouts before?"

"Blackouts?"

"Yes, times when you've woken up, and you haven't remembered how you got somewhere?"

"Yes." His breathing rippled out in short little puffs, as if he was growing distressed.

"Do you always wake up on the beach?"

"Yeah. Richard likes it there, especially the cliffs."

"What are you doing when you wake up?" she asked.

He took a long time answering. "I've been sweating like I'd been running. And twice, I …my fingers had blood on them."

Claire froze, then reminded herself that he could see her reactions. Was he watching? Taunting her to guess his identity?

Or was she wrong to suspect him as the killer?

"Perhaps Richie knows," she finally said in a low soothing voice. "Can I talk to him? Maybe he can tell us what Richard's been doing on the beach."

An eerie quiet descended over the room. Wheaton's

clothing rustled as he shifted, then his breathing changed more dramatically. Finally he stood, paced to the window, his steps hurried and clipped. "Richie?"

"Yeah, it's me."

"Hi, I was hoping you'd visit me today."

"Why?" His voice taunted her. "You like me the best, Dr. Kos?"

"I want to help all of you," Claire said, choosing her words carefully.

"But you like Richie 'cause he's got guts. He takes care of his women, don't he? Women want men to take care of them."

Claire wasn't sure how he interpreted the word "care" so she let the comment slide. "Tell me, Richie, did you take care of your mother?"

A nasty laugh escaped him. "Yeah, I took care of her. She ain't no bad girl anymore."

His tone sent a chill through Claire all the way to her bones. Was it the same voice she'd heard the night before on the phone? Last night, it had sounded muffled. "Did you kill your mother, Richie?"

He grunted. "Someone had to stop her."

"What about those other women? Do you make them pay for what your mother did?"

"The women Richard dates?" He drummed his fingernails on the window sill. "Sometimes, they have to be punished."

"How do you punish them?"

"Richard will kill me if I tell," Richie replied. "He doesn't want to get in trouble."

"In trouble with the police, you mean?"

"Yeah." The nasty laugh rippled out again. "But those bad women get what they deserve."

Claire inhaled. "Does Richard have a girlfriend now?"

"Of course, Doc. He's hung up on you." Another laugh. "Or are you too blind to see it?"

Claire's heartbeat drummed faster. Richard Wheaton had never insinuated he had personal feelings for her, not even once. But she hadn't been able to see him. He could have been looking at her with interest for months, and she hadn't detected it. "Tell me about the beach and what Richard does at night. Does he take women there?"

"Yeah, he gets hot thinking about them."

Claire sensed she was close to the truth. Just a little push and Richie would spill all. But it could be dangerous.

"Is he killing them, Richie? Just like you killed your mother?"

He paced across the room toward her, and Claire tensed.

"Is Richard killing those women on the beach like you killed your mother?"

Suddenly, he bellowed and vaulted toward her. Claire lurched backward, but he caught her and wrapped his hands around her throat. "Shut up, you're gonna get us in trouble!"

"Richie, stop it!" She grabbed his hands and struggled to pull free, but he tightened his fingers around her neck and squeezed harder.

"They deserve it," he cried. "Every one of them. She

killed my sister and buried her in the backyard. Now they have to pay."

Claire cried out, reached for her panic button, but she was disoriented and missed. He dug his nails into her throat so tightly she couldn't breathe. Her legs buckled as she tried to scream....

Chapter Fourteen

Mark was frustrated. His visit with the head of the support group had offered nothing but a dead end. Apparently Al Hogan had dropped out of the group shortly after Claire had, and none of the other members remembered much about him.

As soon as he entered Claire's outer office, he heard her cry. Claire's secretary glanced at him in panic.

"Call security!"

She grabbed the phone, and he removed his Glock, then flung open the door, his heart stopping at the sight of Richard Wheaton choking Claire. She swayed, clawing at his hands.

Mark aimed his gun. "Let her go, Wheaton."

The man jerked his head around, then shoved Claire in front of him. "Get out of my way. She deserves to die."

"No, she's your doctor. She's trying to help you."

"She's just like the others. She wants Richard to go to jail, but I can't let that happen."

"Look, no one's going to jail right now. I'm putting my gun down. Let's talk."

Wheaton's eyes flashed with distrust as he contemplated his next move. But his hands loosened slightly, and Claire coughed, gasping for air.

"Now, let her go. You don't want to hurt Dr. Kos."

Wheaton staggered slightly, an almost gurgling sound erupting from his throat. "She can't tell them what Richie does. She's not supposed to tell."

"I...won't," Claire whispered.

"I don't believe you. You want Richie in jail for killing those women. He goes to the beach. He makes them pay." The man turned a crazed look on Claire, wringing his hands into her neck, and Mark lunged forward, karate-chopped his right arm so hard Wheaton buckled and dropped his grip. Mark knocked him against the wall.

Two security guards raced in. "Throw me some cuffs."

Claire was trying to stand, gasping for air and clutching at a nearby chair.

The guards secured Wheaton, and Mark rushed to help Claire. She clung to his arms as he helped her upright.

"Don't hurt him," Claire whispered in a shaky voice.

"Are you all right?" Mark tilted her head back, examining the red-rimmed bruises on her neck. He glared at Wheaton. "You'll be sorry you touched her, Wheaton."

"Mark..." Claire gripped his arm. "He's ill. It's not his fault."

"He tried to kill you, and he murdered three other women. If it's not his fault, then who the hell is it?"

"His parents," she said in a shaky voice. "They abused him."

"And he turned that abuse into violence against others," Mark said. "That may be the reason, but it doesn't excuse murder. And it certainly won't bring back the victims."

THE NEXT COUPLE of hours went by in a haze for Claire. Detectives Black and Fox arrived along with Dr. Ferguson, and she gave her statement. Wheaton had been taken into custody. Claire had promised Richard she would visit him later, and vowed to follow up and make certain he received the necessary medical and psychiatric treatment.

"He's suffering from dissociative identity disorder," she explained to Detective Black. "It's rare, but occurs when a child endures prolonged childhood abuse and/or trauma." She hesitated, protective feelings emerging. "I'd say watching your mother kill your father could be pretty traumatic. I also suspect she may have killed his little sister and buried her in the backyard."

Black arched a brow. "We'll check out the sister. The police suspected he killed his mother, but they never found proof."

"He's a very disturbed man," Claire said. "He belongs in a psychiatric ward, not a prison."

"If I'd known he was dangerous," Dr. Ferguson said, "you wouldn't have consulted with him alone, Claire."

"We'll let the judge decide what to do with him," Black said.

"At least he'll be off the streets so he can't hurt anyone else," Mark added. "That's what's important."

Claire stiffened when he tried to touch her. She still felt violated by Mark prying into her personal files. There was so much history and pain between them.

Besides, Dr. Ferguson's comments had irritated her as well. He wouldn't have spoken to a male colleague in that tone or implied he needed a bodyguard with a patient.

"I'm going with the detectives. I want to be present when he's interrogated," Mark said. "But I'll drop you off first, Claire."

"Security will drive her," Dr. Ferguson said. "I'd do it myself, Claire, but I have a patient in a few minutes."

"That's not necessary. I'll give her a ride." Kurt Lassiter's voice echoed from the doorway as he rushed to Claire's side. "Good God, Claire, I heard about Wheaton. I'm so sorry."

Claire nodded, twining her hands in her lap as he knelt beside her. She wasn't accustomed to having men hover around her. And now she had three who seemed to be fighting for her attention. "I'm fine, but I feel so bad for Richard."

"Don't, Claire," Mark said.

Claire's head snapped up. *Don't feel bad for him or don't go with Kurt?*

She bit her tongue to stifle a reply. She did feel badly for Richard; she felt as if she'd failed him, just as she'd failed those women, and Mark.

"Claire, call me if you need anything," Dr. Ferguson offered.

"Thanks."

"Come on, Claire, we can talk while I drive you home," Kurt said. "That is, assuming you're finished, Detectives?"

"We are for now," Detective Black said.

"*We're* not," Mark answered.

Claire heard the undertones in his voice, but the idea of him sneaking around and asking about her condition still disturbed her. She didn't want Mark's pity or a love based on guilt or responsibility.

"If you need me, I'll be at home," she said. "I have to discuss Richard's treatment with Kurt so I'll ride with him."

Kurt's smooth hand slid over hers, and Claire forced herself not to tense. Mark didn't bother to reply. She heard his clipped heels as he strode out the door.

But she held her chin high as she left the office. She had survived the past year without Mark. She could do it once more. She only wished she hadn't given her heart to him. Because this time he would take it with him when he left.

And she would never love again.

CLAIRE WAS completely shutting him out of her life. The fact that she was leaving with Kurt Lassiter intensified Mark's emotions.

She could not go from his bed to another man's.

Not his Claire.

She's not your Claire. You deserted her when she needed you the most.

How could she ever forgive him for that? How could he ever forgive himself?

He followed Detectives Black and Fox to the precinct where he met up with Agent Devlin.

"He confessed?" Devlin asked.

"In a roundabout way," Detective Black said. "We've put him in an interrogation room."

"We're getting a search warrant for his place to look for corroborating evidence," Detective Fox added.

"I'd like to be there," Devlin said. "We need to search for trophies, see if he kept something from the victims."

Fox nodded. "We'll start the questioning."

Black and Fox both entered the interrogation room while Devlin and Mark watched through the two-way mirror. Mark was shocked at the change in Wheaton's demeanor. The angry man who'd shouted obscenities and attacked Claire had disappeared. Instead of fighting and yelling, Wheaton had withdrawn into a shell. He sat in the chair with his knees drawn up to his chin, wrapped his arms around his legs and rocked himself back and forth.

"I didn't do anything wrong," he whispered in a childlike voice. "Please don't hurt me."

"What kind of game is he playing?" Devlin asked.

"He's mentally ill," Mark said. "Claire said he's suffering from dissociative identity disorder. Split personalities."

"Dammit," Devlin snarled. "We may never get a solid confession out of him."

"True," Mark said. "But maybe we'll find evidence at his place to incriminate him." He had to be the killer. So far, all the other employees at CIRP, right down to the repairmen, had checked out or had alibis.

"Let's hope so," Devlin said. "Otherwise, we're going to need Claire to come back in to question him—"

"We're leaving Claire out of it from now on. She's been through enough."

Devlin gave him an odd look, full of questions that Mark refused to answer. Maybe because he didn't know the answers yet himself.

"The court-appointed psychiatrist can take over," Mark said. "I won't have Claire put in any more danger by that maniac."

ALTHOUGH CLAIRE knew she was out of danger, she still felt uneasy with Kurt Lassiter as they drove to her cottage. He was too intense. And he wanted more than she could offer.

Oblivious to her discomfort, he questioned her about the ordeal with Richard Wheaton. Claire conveyed the details, trying for a detached tone, but the quiver in her voice betrayed her bravado.

When he parked and killed the engine, she reached for the door handle, hoping he'd take the hint and leave.

"I'm walking you in, Claire. I want to make sure you're safe."

She started to argue but he jumped out of the car and was at her door in seconds.

"I wish I'd been in there with you and Wheaton, Claire." He pressed a hand to her back as they entered her cottage, and Claire tensed again, thinking of Mark and how natural the protective gesture felt. With Kurt, it didn't seem natural at all.

"You won't interview him again without a second doctor present," Kurt said.

She frowned. "Wheaton might not respond with someone else, Kurt."

"It doesn't matter. That's one point Ferguson and I agree on."

"I didn't realize you disagreed on other things," Claire said.

Kurt cleared his throat. "We've had a difference of opinion on some treatments and a bit of research he's doing, nothing major."

Claire frowned, wondering what he meant, but she was too exhausted to explore the issue. Besides, she didn't want to encourage Kurt to stay any longer.

"Thanks for the ride."

He moved nearer to her, so close she smelled his aftershave, a musky blend that seemed stronger today. "You know I'd do anything to protect you, Claire."

"I'm fine," Claire said. "Maybe life can return to normal now."

"I hope so," Kurt said. "Then we can pursue a relationship. Maybe we could spend time together away from the office. Take a long weekend trip."

Claire inhaled, reluctant to hurt him, but unable to envision herself with Kurt. Mark's questions about Kurt getting rough with one of his patients surfaced, too, although she didn't know why. She hadn't believed the accusations at the time, yet she felt undercurrents of anger from Kurt now, as if he might snap if she refused him. "Kurt—"

"Shh." He pressed his finger to her lips to silence her.

"You don't have to make a decision this minute. Give us a chance to get to know one another." He dropped his finger and cradled her hand in his. "I'm a good dancer, Claire. I like to sail and go to the opera. I could show you a good time."

She shook her head slowly, knowing there was no use. Her heart belonged to one man, even though he had broken it. "I'm sorry, Kurt, I…I don't want to lead you on. I'm not interested in being anything other than friends."

His fingers tightened around her hand. "It's because of that agent isn't it? Steele?"

"Kurt—"

"There's something between you two, isn't there?"

He was hurting her wrist. "We have some history, but it's over."

"Then why won't you see me, Claire?" His voice turned cold, angry. "I've been patient—"

"I know, and I'm sorry." She pulled away, wrapped her arms around her waist. "I just can't, Kurt."

"It's not over between us, Claire." His voice was so harsh that Claire stepped backward, bracing herself in case he got physical.

But thankfully, he turned and stalked out the door. Claire locked it behind him, then sagged onto the couch, grateful he was gone. Now the killer had been caught, she could relax. And Mark could go on to another case.

But after loving him again, how could she continue alone?

"DID YOU FIND ANYTHING?" Mark asked.

Agent Devlin glanced up, his eyebrows arched.

"Some adult magazines and sex toys, which only proves he's a male with a sexual appetite, not a murderer."

They had been searching Wheaton's apartment for over an hour. The place looked as if two different people lived in it. The kitchen was immaculate, the cupboards tidy, the refrigerator well stocked, whereas the bedroom looked as if a hurricane had blown through. Clothes, magazines, newsletters from some underground group of white male extremists and adult videos littered the floor. And in the closet, they'd even found a small rag doll, its thumbs worn and damp as if someone had been chewing on the ends.

Mark frowned. They had expected some kind of shrine to Claire, at least pictures or the other scarves he had stolen from her cottage.

"No souvenirs from the victims?"

"Not unless there's a secret room somewhere."

Mark checked the closet, reached up and removed a shoe box from the top shelf. "Anybody check out his car?"

"Black and Fox did when they impounded it after they brought him in. Zilch. No scarves or souvenirs, although they're checking it for DNA."

A clipping of Wheaton's father's murder lay in the box, along with clippings about his mother's death and the death of his younger sister. In the first picture, Wheaton was a little boy, only five. In the second, an angry adolescent wearing black leather and chains.

Another article had been included, this one described Claire's lecture tour across country.

"His sneakers are filled with sand," Devlin said. "Which proves he was at the beach. At least it's something."

But it didn't necessarily prove he was a killer. Mark didn't like it. He'd thought they'd find enough evidence so they could close the case.

Something was still bothering him. Something about the support group maybe? Or Lassiter…

Or was he just looking for a way to keep the case open so he'd have an excuse to stay close to Claire?

CLAIRE HAD JUST closed her eyes for a brief nap before the show when she heard the first whisper.

"You've been a bad girl, Claire."

She froze and gripped the bedcovers, her heart pounding in her chest. No…she'd imagined it. She'd been dreaming.

"Bad girls have to be punished. Why couldn't you save yourself for me?"

A deep trembling started within her as she reached for the phone. *Save yourself.* The first time the killer had murmured those words she'd thought he was warning her to save herself from danger. Now she understood the true meaning.

He knew she had slept with Mark, and he was going to punish her.

She had to call for help.

She lunged for the phone, but a hand snaked out and knocked it from her hand. Then a man dove on top of her. She bucked upward, throwing up her hands to fend him off, but he pressed a hand over her mouth, and the sharp point of a needle stabbed her arm.

The killer had drugged the other women before he'd killed them.

"No!" She thrashed and kicked, but her cries faded into a silent plea, darkness surrounding her as she sank into nothingness.

Chapter Fifteen

By the time Mark finished, it was time for Claire's show to begin. He had called her cottage to offer her a ride, but she didn't answer, so he assumed she'd stayed at the hospital to talk to Lassiter. Or maybe she'd already gone to the station for the evening show. Knowing Claire, she'd refuse to take the night off.

He turned on the radio, hoping to hear her voice, to know she was safe.

"Folks, tonight, we're switching from our normal programming."

Mark frowned at the sound of Drew's voice.

"Dr. Kos is taking the night off, so we're running a short segment on the best of the *Calling Claire* show, then featuring a special request hour of your favorite music."

Mark's uneasiness mounted. He dialed Claire's home again, but she didn't answer, so he called the radio station and asked to speak to Drew.

"Where's Claire?"

"Hell if I know," Drew said. "She didn't show up."

The hairs on the back of his neck prickled. "She didn't call?"

"No, I haven't heard a word. That's not like Claire, either," Drew said. "I heard you guys caught the Midnight Murderer today."

"We think so," Mark said, although his gut warned him not to jump the gun, especially knowing Claire hadn't shown up at the station. Something didn't feel right.

"Call me if you hear from her. I'll phone her office and the detectives we met with today. She might have gotten tied up with a patient." Like the one they'd arrested. Claire had been so worried about him, maybe she'd gone to visit him at the jail.

A few minutes later, sheer panic had taken hold. She was not at the police precinct. Neither Black nor Fox had heard from her. And she hadn't returned to her office. He finally got through to Lassiter's secretary, but Lassiter hadn't returned to the hospital after driving Claire home.

"Give me his home phone and cell phone," Mark said.

"Sir, I can't release that information."

"This is Agent Mark Steele of the FBI. It's an emergency. Dr. Kos may be missing. He might have information about her whereabouts."

"Well, er…" She hesitated. "I suppose it would be all right."

Five minutes later he had Lassiter on the line.

"I left Claire at the house," Lassiter said, although his voice sounded bitter.

"You'd better be telling me the truth." Mark slammed down the phone and drove like a maniac to Claire's cottage. He knocked, praying she'd been asleep and hadn't heard the phone, but pushed open the door. It was unlocked. His heart pounded.

Unholstering his gun, he scanned the room, but found it empty. Then he inched back to the bedroom. The bed covers had been tousled.

A hypodermic lay on the floor.

Dear God, Wheaton wasn't the serial killer. There was someone else.

And whoever he was, he had Claire.

WHERE WAS SHE?

Claire opened her eyes, but the black hole of emptiness she'd lived in for the past year had grown into an endless dark pit. She struggled to free herself, but she'd been bound and gagged, the ropes cutting off her circulation. A rocking motion sent a wave of dizziness through her, and the scent of salt water and that odd odor permeated her nostrils. A spray of water misted her face. She was on a boat. A fairly small one.

"We should have been together, Claire," he said in a whispery voice. "You should have saved yourself for me. I knew all your secrets, but I didn't care. I loved you anyway. Even if you weren't perfect."

She wanted to cry out that she was sorry, that she would help him because she knew he was ill, he had to be, but her throat closed. Tears filled her eyes and trickled down her cheeks.

He slid a finger over her cheek and caught one on

his finger. "Don't cry, Claire. You know bad girls have to be punished."

Panic warred with despair in her chest as her life flashed before her. Or the life she might have had if she and Mark could have forgiven each other for their mistakes.

If she hadn't given up on love.

Who was this man? His voice sounded familiar, as if she knew him, yet not familiar at all. Maybe he'd disguised it.

"But you chose Steele. Even after he abandoned you, you ran back to him the minute he came to town."

She loved him. She'd always loved him. And she could never love anyone else. But he wanted her to fight for her sight, and she wasn't sure she could. She would never be perfect enough....

"I didn't mind that you were blind, you know," he said in a small voice. "Because you could see me for what I am. You looked past the scars and saw the man inside."

More tears choked her, but she swallowed them back. If only he'd remove the gag so she could talk to him. She inhaled again and smelled that odd odor. Mark had said it was an ointment for insect bites and rashes. But this man reeked of the smell—what was wrong with him?

"He should suffer, too, for what he did to you," he said, his voice rising in pitch. "Yes, we'll call him, Claire. He should know what he lost by running out on you."

Claire shook her head wildly. If he called Mark, he would come running to protect her. He'd walk into a trap. She couldn't let anything happen to him.

"Shh." He pressed a damp, sweaty finger to her lips. "It'll be all right, sweetheart. I'm going to take care of everything."

Claire shook her head again and tried to scream, but the gag caught the sound and muffled her cry to a gurgle. She had to think of a way out, a way to save Mark before they both ended up dead.

"HELLO, LIEUTENANT. Claire's been a bad girl."

Mark gripped the phone, his throat constricting.

"She should have chosen me over you," he whispered, "and now she has to pay."

"Who is this?"

"You told me how wonderful she was, and you were right," he murmured. "Her hair is like sunshine, her lips like strawberries. And now she's finally going to be mine."

What did he mean? Mark had told him how wonderful she was?

The killer was someone Mark knew? Had he kidnapped Claire to get revenge on Mark?

God. Had they been chasing their tails, looking at false leads and running in circles the entire time?

Rage filled him. "Where have you taken her?"

"Away from you. You don't deserve her."

"Maybe not," Mark said in a dark voice. "But she doesn't deserve to be hurt, either."

"You should have stayed away from her," he said in an eerie voice. "It's all your fault that she was bad. You came back, and she forgot about me."

Mark had to keep him talking. To get some clue to

his identity. "How did you meet Claire? Are you one of her patients?"

A bitter laugh escaped the man. "No. But we shared our secrets. And now we're going to share even more."

The phone suddenly went dead. Mark closed his eyes at the insanity in the man's voice, his imagination going wild. The man was sick. And he was obviously obsessed with Claire.

What was he going to do to her?

Taking several deep breaths to calm his panic and banish the horrifying images flashing into his mind, he punched in Devlin's number. He had to figure out the connection, how the killer knew both him and Claire.

Devlin answered on the third ring. Mark explained the call, the clues clicking into place. "He said he knew Claire's secrets. It must be the man she met in that support group."

"I've been looking into the names on that list."

"Did you find something?"

"According to the links I found on the first victim's computer, she belonged to an online support group."

Mark's fingers tightened around the handset.

"So I checked the other vics' computers, and all three belonged to online support groups."

"That's how he chose his victims. In a support group, people felt safe, they could disclose all their secrets." Mark inhaled sharply. Damn. "Cross-check the name of the veteran in the group Claire attended with the ones who visited the online groups."

"I'm on it."

Mark glanced at his watch, the killer's threats reverberating in his head. Every second they took might be too long. "Make it fast, Devlin. I don't know how long this maniac will keep Claire alive."

Or what he might do to her before he killed her.

CLAIRE'S PULSE raced as her kidnapper jerked her up from the boat, then pushed her up the embankment. Where was he taking her now? Why hadn't he killed her while they were in the boat and dumped her body overboard? Was he going to kill her now? Or wait until Mark arrived and force him to watch?

That is, *if* Mark arrived. How would he know where to find them?

Her foot hit a tangle of brush, and she nearly stumbled, but he caught her. The feel of his hands made her skin crawl. A minute later, he shoved her into what she assumed was a house or cabin. Ocean waves crashed against the rocks in a violent frenzy. The air was salty, humid. A seashell crunched below the man's boots. They were on the beach, but she had no idea where. Had he carried her to his place? An abandoned house maybe?

He led her through the room to another, and she struggled to get her bearings, but she was so disoriented. The room smelled musty, like cigarettes and stale beer. And that ointment. Had he been sick recently? In the hospital? Had she met him in the psychiatric ward? Mark had checked Dr. Lassiter and Ferguson's patients, hadn't he?

Finally, he pushed her into a chair, and removed the gag.

"Where are we?"

"We're at my place, Claire."

"Let me go, and I can help you," Claire said, trying desperately to buy time.

"No, it's too late."

Claire cringed inwardly. "But I'll tell them you need help," she said, "I can testify and recommend therapy—"

"I went to therapy," he said, his tone sharp. "But it didn't help. I tried to make friends with you, but you ran away from me."

"I…what? I would never turn away a patient."

"I wasn't your patient! I wanted to be your friend."

Claire suddenly placed the voice, searching her memory banks for his name. "You're the man from the support group? Al Hogan?"

"You finally remember. See, you did notice me." His breath whisked out, his voice sounding relieved and disturbed at the same time. "But you deserted me. Why did you have to run, Claire?" He whimpered, and she realized he was on the verge of hysteria.

"I was in a bad place back then," Claire said, remembering how difficult it had been for her to cope with all she'd lost. "It had nothing to do with you. Please believe me. I wasn't ready for a relationship with anyone."

"But I came to you before the accident. Steele told me to see you. I thought…I thought you'd help me."

Claire's head ached as she tried to follow his logic. He was pacing the room then, his heels clicking on the linoleum. They squeaked when he walked, his tone vacillating between eerily calm and irrational.

"You came to my office because of Mark?"

"Yes," his breathing grew more erratic. "But the minute I arrived, you ran off to the airport…you were driving in that storm…" his voice cracked. "I tried to stop you."

"To stop me? Where?"

"Outside, I yelled for you, but you were so infatuated with him, you left. Then I followed you."

The memories surfaced, painful but clear. The blinding lights… "You were driving behind me?"

"Yes, I followed you and tried to get you to stop, but that truck came along," his voice rose again, and Claire's stomach rolled. So, her accident hadn't entirely been an accident.

"I couldn't see because of your bright headlights," she whispered.

"I didn't mean for that to happen," his voice warbled, "but I had to stop you. I couldn't let you marry him, not when I wanted you."

"But I didn't know you then. I was suffering myself, don't you understand? You can't hold people accountable for their actions when they're in pain."

He stroked her hair, and Claire's insides revolted. "After the accident, I wanted to help you, Claire," he whispered, "to hold you and comfort you." He twisted a strand around his finger, then moved so close his breath brushed her cheek. The odd odor nearly suffocated her.

"But you didn't give me a chance. When I went to that support group, I tried to befriend you, but you refused to even have coffee with me."

She had rebuked him twice. Unknowingly, of course, but he obviously had fixated on her, and in his eyes, she had hurt him.

"I'm sorry," Claire whispered. "I'm really sorry, I didn't know how you felt, but let me help you now."

"There's no turning back," he said in a monotone, his voice fading off with hopeless despair. "It's too late for both of us."

AN HOUR LATER, Agent Devlin phoned Mark. He had been pacing the confines of Claire's cottage, praying for a miracle. "The name Al Hogan came up on all three computer files," Devlin said.

Mark frowned. Hogan had also attended the support group with Claire. But how did he know Mark?

"Report says he was suffering from posttraumatic stress disorder related to a stint he did in Desert Storm. He was pulled out of some rubble following an explosion—"

"Jeez." Mark gripped the edge of the coffee table. "I rescued the man. He was incoherent, had some damage to one of his legs. He thought he'd probably lose it and begged me to leave him to die."

"You're sure it's the same guy?"

"Positive," Mark said. "I remember telling him about Claire, that I was going to propose to her when I returned stateside, and then suggested he find a good therapist to help him."

"He must have come looking for her."

"He wasn't listed as a patient of hers."

"He met her at the support group. That's what he

meant when he said she'd shared her secrets with him."
Mark rubbed a hand over his face. "Claire told everyone at the group about the accident and…" The baby.
Mark exhaled. "And he probably tried to befriend the
other women in the online support groups, but they
turned him down. Now, he blames Claire."

"If it is the same guy, maybe we caught a break." The
papers rustled as Devlin fished through the file. "He has
a local address on Catcall Island."

It made sense. "Near the water, where he has easy
access to the beach."

"I'll phone the locals, issue an APB for him," Devlin said.

"And I'll check out the address."

"He's got an alias, Arden Holland."

Mark shook his head in disbelief. "The damn janitor. He's been right under our noses. But he must have
disguised himself. I didn't recognize him." Then again,
he'd only passed the man a couple of times, and he'd
kept his head down while he swept. Claire hadn't even
considered him a suspect. Obviously, he'd worn a disguise. And he wasn't as old as he claimed or appeared.

"Call the locals for backup," Devlin ordered.

Mark nodded, although he was already out the door.
He couldn't waste another minute. He had to find
Claire.

CLAIRE ATTEMPTED to calm Al Hogan, but the man
slipped in and out of reality. One minute, his cries were
that of a tormented man, the next, his voice full of anger
and vengeance.

"You were in the war, weren't you?" Claire asked. "Isn't that why you attended the support group?"

"Yes, and things happened over there, things that no one talks about."

Claire shivered at his tone. "I'd like to hear about them, Al. I'm a good listener."

"I thought my girl back home was going to wait for me," he whispered, "but she took one look at me when I was discharged and freaked. She couldn't handle the scars."

"Were you injured in combat?"

A bitter sound rushed out, part laugh, part cry.

Claire wished she could see his face, find out what the woman had seen so she could know how to deal with him. "Untie me and let me touch you," she whispered. "Maybe I can soothe away the pain of her words."

He went utterly still, and she held her breath, hoping he would play into her hands. It was the only chance she had.

"Please, I don't know what happened, but your scars won't bother me."

He slowly moved toward her, and she inhaled, praying she could find the strength and calm to comfort him and talk him out of this craziness, but suddenly a loud crashing sound exploded behind her. A gunshot rang out.

She pushed herself upright to stand, but Hogan shoved her backward, and she fell, slamming into the wall.

"Stay down, Claire," Mark yelled. Then another shot

pinged through the air. A loud thump followed—a body had hit the floor.

Oh, God, had Mark been shot?

Chapter Sixteen

Mark hadn't seen the gun. He rolled sideways, pressed a hand to his shoulder and tried to get his bearings. When he'd first looked through the window and spotted Claire tied up with that maniac screeching and pacing in front of her, he'd nearly lost his cool. It had taken every ounce of restraint he possessed to wait until an opportune moment to burst in.

Blood oozed from his arm, and pain knifed through him, but he ignored it and reached for his gun on the floor. Hogan kicked him in the chin and sent him bouncing backward. Mark grunted and saw stars, then crouched into an attack mode, but Hogan was fast, and the butt of his gun slammed against Mark's head. He went down, struggling not to pass out, but darkness descended, trapping him in its clutches.

Maybe a half hour later, Mark stirred, his head spinning, his shoulder aching. He blinked back the sweat that had trickled down his forehead into his eyes, furious that Hogan had gotten the better of him and had tied him to a chair.

"Mark?" Claire cried. "Mark, can you hear me? Please wake up."

"I'm here, Claire," he whispered. "Hold on, sweetheart—"

"She's not your sweetheart anymore," Hogan muttered. "She's mine."

Mark grimaced at the wild-eyed look in the man's thin face. His skin was blotchy red, his pallor a pasty yellow.

"I don't belong to anyone," Claire said in a surprisingly calm voice. Mark realized she'd probably been stalling for time by encouraging Hogan to talk. He had to do the same thing, give Black time to get his message and send backup.

"Why are you doing this, Hogan?" Mark asked.

"Because you don't deserve her."

"That may be true." He slowly maneuvered his hands to untie his restraints. "But Claire hasn't done anything to hurt you."

Hogan's face twisted with rage. "She ran away from me, just like those other women. They don't want me now that I'm not whole."

"You look whole to me," Mark said, although he did appear demented. "I know other men who came out of combat looking much worse. At least you survived, so stop making excuses." Hopefully, Mark could make him angry enough to snap him out of his self-pity.

His attempt backfired. Hogan raised the gun and slammed it across Mark's temple. Mark's head rolled backward. He bit his tongue and tasted blood.

"You think you know everything," Hogan said. "But you don't. You didn't know Claire had lost your child."

Mark's chest squeezed. "No, but that wouldn't have changed things for me."

Claire's breath hitched. He hoped she understood that he meant it.

"But her sight loss—how would that have changed your feelings?" Hogan paced over to Claire, then traced a thumb down her cheek. Claire breathed in deeply, but reined in her control and managed not to flinch. Mark couldn't control his rage though. He nearly bolted up from the chair.

"I know how people act when they think you're different, Claire," Hogan said. "You didn't tell Steele because you knew he wouldn't want an imperfect wife."

"She was wrong," Mark said, unweaving the knots. "I'm here now, aren't I?"

"You came for me," Hogan said simply. Then he turned to Claire. "You know I'm different. I can accept your blindness. In fact, I understand the reason you can't see, and I can help you."

He knelt beside her, and twisted a strand of hair around his finger. Fury shot through Mark. "You can't stand to look at yourself now, because you blame yourself for that accident."

Claire's lower lip trembled.

"You blame yourself because you were careless. You ignored the storm just so you could chase after Steele when he was leaving you and your baby behind."

"He didn't know I was pregnant," Claire whispered. "But I wanted him to…in case."

In case he didn't come back.

Mark's heart broke. For both of them and all they had lost.

"You told yourself a thousand times that you shouldn't have driven in the rain," Hogan taunted. "Your baby would be alive today if you hadn't been so foolish. So now, you don't want to see yourself. That's why you're blind. You like living in the darkness—it's your way of punishing yourself."

Claire shook her head back and forth, a tear escaping, then getting trapped in a strand of hair lying against her cheek.

Mark's throat closed. So that was the reason Claire hadn't tried to see another doctor. Hogan was right— she was punishing herself. Mark ached to reach out, drag her into his arms and absolve her guilt.

"You knew you were losing the baby when the car went into the river, that's why you begged me not to save you." He wheezed. "I understood that, too, Claire."

Mark's head snapped up. "What?"

"Yes," Hogan said, swinging his gaze toward Mark. "I was there. I dragged Claire out of the water and called the paramedics."

"You were following her?"

"Yes," Claire cried. "His headlights blinded me."

The man's taunting song, "Blinded by the light," suddenly made sense.

So Hogan had saved Claire's life. How sick was he? Had he caused her accident, too?

A rage unlike anything he'd ever known splintered

through Mark. Hogan's obsession had cost Claire her sight and their child.

Somehow, he had to save Claire and make her realize that none of this was her fault.

Hogan reached over and removed a hypodermic from the scarred wooden table.

"What's that for?" Mark asked.

Hogan wiped Claire's arm, then raised the needle. "So Claire won't suffer anymore. Neither of us will."

Mark gritted his teeth and slid the last strand of rope from its knot. He saw a second hypodermic on the table. Was Hogan planning a murder/suicide? Or did he intend the shot for Mark?

Determination and anger driving him, Mark suddenly lunged at Hogan and knocked the shot from his hand. Hogan reached for his gun, but Mark rammed a fist into his gut. Hogan buckled. Mark dove for the gun, but Hogan kicked his wounded shoulder, sending him staggering backward. Then Hogan picked up the gun, aimed it at Mark's chest and fired again.

Mark's body flew backward as the bullet pierced his chest. He'd let his men down and lost them, and now he'd failed Claire. Again.

And this time it would cost them their lives.

CLAIRE CRIED OUT, panic robbing her of breath. "Mark?"

He groaned and she realized he'd been shot again. How bad was it? She wished she could see him so she'd know...

"Please stop this, Al," Claire pleaded. "Please, let me help you. No one else needs to die."

"I told you it's too late," Hogan mumbled.

Claire struggled against her ties, but the sharp point of a needle pierced her arm. She tried to fight the effects of the drug but they slowly seeped into her system, blurring her senses and deflating her strength. When Hogan lifted her in his arms and began to carry her outside, she was barely cognizant of the motion.

She remembered the way the other women had been found. She only hoped that somehow Mark managed to survive. If she'd only regained her sight, maybe she could have helped them somehow.

The wind brushed her cheek, the salty air filtering through the haze of her fear as Hogan walked toward the ocean. His steps were unsteady, as if his feet kept slipping in the sand, and she realized that he dragged one leg behind him. A brief memory surfaced of a man carrying her from the river. Al Hogan had rescued her from drowning the same day he'd destroyed her life by causing her accident. But now he intended to end her life.

So much had happened in between.

She had thought she'd lost Mark, but then he'd returned. An image of his tall, muscular body, and his handsome face flashed into her mind. She wished she could see him, touch him one more time before she left the world.

She wanted to tell him that she loved him.

Hogan stopped and whispered a few words, although Claire couldn't understand his mutterings. Then he rubbed something soft against her cheek. A rose petal; the delicate fragrance now seemed pungent.

Tears drifted down her cheeks. She didn't want to die. She wanted another chance to make everything right with Mark.

But Hogan lowered her to the ground, then she felt the soft fabric of a scarf slipping around her neck....

MARK ROUSED HIMSELF by sheer will, his heart racing when he realized Claire was gone. Where had Hogan taken her?

To the beach...

Dear God. Fear clouded his brain, mingling with the pain from the bullet wounds. But he jerked the dish-cloth off the table, pressed it against the blood seeping from his chest, grabbed his gun, and staggered upright. Holding on to the wall for support, he groped his way through the open screen door, stumbling down the dark-ened path to the beach. Loose sand and wild sea oats complicated his journey, but he trudged forward. He couldn't stop. He couldn't pass out. Not yet. He had to save Claire.

Nothing mattered except getting to Claire right now. What had happened to Hogan to drive him to this point? Mark had lost his own men, had thought he couldn't survive that tragedy.

Now he had a second chance, someone else to care for. He couldn't lose Claire again. Especially to a crazy man like Hogan.

Forcing one foot in front of the other, he squinted through the darkness, searching the beach for Hogan and Claire. A shadow moved in the distance. He spot-ted them. Hogan was bending over Claire.

Mark ran, stumbling, battling to remain conscious until he reached the brush surrounding the area. Hogan pivoted to search behind him. Mark ducked behind the sea oats, hoping for a clear shot. If Hogan would only move away from Claire…

His opportunity came a second later. Hogan kicked some underbrush aside, then positioned Claire's head on a thick patch of sea oats as if it was a pillow. He held his breath that Claire was all right, that the drugs he'd given her hadn't already killed her, but it was too dark to judge if she was breathing. Then he noticed the scarf. Hogan had already slipped it around her neck.

Was he too late?

He aimed to kill, but Hogan kept weaving back and forth. What if he hit Claire?

Pure rage pushed Mark forward. He vaulted out of the brush like a madman and fired, catching Hogan in the shoulder. Damn, he'd meant to kill him.

Hogan was amazingly quick. He threw up a fist and knocked the gun from Mark's hands. The two of them hit the dirt, rolling, fighting, struggling. They traded blow for blow, resorting to the marital arts training they'd both used in the military. Mark flipped Hogan off of him, rolled to his back, then kicked upward, catching Hogan in his weak knee. Hogan flew backward, and Mark grabbed his Glock, then fired again, this time his shot on target.

Hogan's body bounced backward with the impact. He grabbed his chest, blood spurting. His eyes went wide with fear, but a second later, a calmness fell over his features. Then Hogan took a step backward. Mark realized his intentions and crawled forward to save him, but Hogan stepped off the ledge and fell into the ocean. His final cry echoed in the wind as the waves swallowed his body.

Mark dragged himself toward Claire, weak and dizzy. He was losing more blood now, but he had to make it. Another inch. Then another. Close the distance. Then he could touch her.

His hand found hers. She was still warm. Thank God she was breathing.

Darkness came over him as he collapsed in the sand beside her.

MARK HAD NO IDEA how long he'd been unconscious. But he had to pull himself out of it and see Claire. Hold her. Tell her loved her.

Even if she never wanted to see him again.

He was the reason Hogan had become obsessed with her in the first place. He had set the path of destruction that had almost cost her her life. Twice.

Would she hate him now that it was over?

He groaned and opened his eyes, but it took him several minutes to focus. A blur of white filled his vision, then faded and returned, this time bringing with it a man's face. Devlin.

"Well, hell, I thought I told you to call for backup before you went out to Hogan's place."

A bubble of laughter caught in his chest, but it hurt too damn much to release it. He had to clear his throat twice to find his voice. Then his mouth was so dry his lips practically stuck together. "I did."

"Yeah, but you didn't wait for them."

"No time."

Devlin nodded, a small smile curving his mouth just before he turned serious. "You were in surgery for hours."

So he was in the hospital. How long had he been there? "Did you find Hogan's body?"

Devlin nodded. "Yeah. He had a suspicious rash, the doctors suspect he was exposed to some chemical warfare. CIRP is already researching it."

Mark nodded, but even that movement hurt. "Where's Claire? I want to see her."

"She's in another room."

His tone sent alarm up Mark's aching spine. "She's all right, isn't she?"

Devlin's expression gave nothing away, but his silence did. "She's alive."

He cleared his throat again, pried his parched lips apart, his heart pounding. "What aren't you telling me?"

"You need to rest, Mark. You've just had two bullets removed, the second one came within an inch of piercing your heart."

He didn't give a rat's ass about his injuries. "Tell me about Claire, dammit."

Devlin's gaze shot sideways to the drawn curtains as if they held a reprieve. "She hasn't awakened yet. The dose of Percoset Hogan gave her was pretty strong, and she hit her head."

"How long have I been here?"

"About six hours." Devlin chuckled sardonically. "You were damn lucky, that shrapnel you caught from the war stopped the bullet, making it ricochet away from your heart. Saved your life."

"Claire should have come out of it by now."

"The doctor said it may take time. She suffered a pretty bad shock."

Mark gritted his teeth and tasted sand. "Take me to her." He tried to sit up, but Devlin pushed him back down. "Hold on before you tear something loose."

Mark grabbed Devlin's sleeve. "Either help me, or I'll drag my butt over there myself."

Devlin stared at him long and hard, then nodded. "Let me get a nurse so you don't rip your stitches."

Mark lay back and silently cursed, the minutes between his request and the nurse's arrival dragging by. Finally, a plump woman named Brenda Lou showed up. "I hear you're being stubborn."

"I have to see Claire Kos," Mark said. "She has to know that I love her."

Brenda Lou burst into a big smile. "After my divorce, I thought all the good ones were gone."

Mark hoped Claire saw it that way, too, that somehow he could get through to her.

CLAIRE COULD SEE the red. She had been blind so long, she had shut out the color, but now it was back like a ghost haunting her dreams, only the ghost didn't float in white, it floated in the color of the devil, the color of blood.

Red water swirled around her, choking her. Drowning out her life, taking her baby with her. No, the blood was Mark's. He'd been shot.

He was dead.

And she was lying in the sand. Facedown. A scarf around her neck.

The killer had finally taken everything away she had ever cared for, loved. She welcomed the darkness, shut out the light, the colors, that awful bloodred.

"Claire?"

Mark's voice drifted through the haze. "Claire, wake up, honey. It's all over."

She didn't believe him. He was gone. And she wanted to be with him.

"Claire, don't leave me now, please. I need you." His voice wavered. "I don't care if you never see again, Claire. I don't care, do you hear me? I love you just the way you are. I just want you by my side."

A small burst of light broke through the empty black sea that consumed her. A sliver that shimmered like a falling star begging her to make a wish. She closed her eyes tighter and sank into her thoughts, knowing her wish had to come from the heart.

She wanted to see again, to look into Mark's eyes and find that raw emotion that had once brought them together, the passion that had created their baby.

But wishes didn't come true…she had wished for love and a child before, but she had lost them both…

"PLEASE OPEN THE BLINDS, it's too damn dark in here," Mark said. "I want her to feel the sunshine on her face." Even if she couldn't see it.

"You're right, this room needs a little light." The nurse slid open the white blinds. "Anything else I can do for you, Mr. Steele?"

He had an idea. "Does this hospital have a gift shop?"

She nodded. "Of course. Do you want some flowers?"

"No." He motioned for her to lean closer, then whispered his request in a low voice.

Her dark brows quirked together as she smiled. "All right, I'll be right back." She left, and he picked up Claire's hand, cradling it between his own. She looked so beautiful with her blond curls spread across the white pillow, like an angel asleep for the night. But nightmares haunted his angel, and he wanted to banish them forever.

A few minutes later, the nurse bustled in and pressed the object in his hand. Then she patted his back and walked out. He turned to Claire and whispered her name. Her face looked pale, then her eyes fluttered, and he thought for a moment that she might respond. But she didn't move or open her eyes.

"Claire, you have to wake up. I need you." He dropped his head forward, the pain in his chest nothing compared to the thought of losing her again. "I know I let you down. But none of it was your fault. You were a victim of this crazy man, Hogan." His words came out choked. "You had no way of knowing he'd become obsessed with you, no way of seeing that he'd followed you." No, Mark had actually set those events in motion. "It was my fault, not yours. Please come back to me. Let me make it up to you. We can start over." He envisioned their future, long quiet walks on the beach after work, they could buy a boat and learn to sail, he'd even buy Claire a horse so she could ride again. They could finally take that bareback ride together.

"If you can forgive me, we can have a life together. I want that, Claire. I don't care if you're blind or not, do you hear me? I just want to be with you."

She stirred slightly, then nestled further into the covers, and he swallowed back his fear. Other emotions rose to the surface, the feelings he'd experienced the day he'd lost his men on the battlefield. The day his best friend had died in his arms.

The emptiness, the pain, the guilt.

He had never been able to talk about that day. But now, he couldn't help himself. The words poured out, along with the terrible self-recriminations he'd lived with since the tragedy. He told her about Marie and Kevin and his visit.

"It was my fault, Claire, I was in charge. I should have figured out that that man was a traitor just like it was my fault that Hogan came after you." His fingers tightened around her hand. "I was trying to help him when I told him about you, trying to give him hope. It never occurred to me that he'd become obsessed with you."

He blinked back tears, releasing emotions he'd suppressed for a long time. "I probably don't deserve another chance, not after all you've been through, but I swear when you wake up, things will be different." He pressed a kiss to her hand, then laid it against her cheek, his voice choked. "I love you, Claire. I want you to be my wife."

He squeezed her hand and pressed the small plastic

picture frame inside her palm. "Remember that little picture frame you bought, the one you were bringing to the airport? Here's a new frame." He cleared his throat. "We'll make another baby, and this time we'll put a picture of our child in it. Then we'll fill the whole damn wall with pictures of our family."

MARRY MARK. Make another baby. Fill the little frame with a picture of their baby, the whole wall with pictures of their family.

Claire wanted to believe that was true. That Mark was really beside her, alive, making promises.

She fought the heavy weighted feeling, and felt the warmth of his palm. He was real. She had heard his heartfelt confessions about losing his men and now understood the terrible guilt that had driven him from the military to the FBI.

She understood about guilt.

Al Hogan had been right.

She had hidden away in a blinding sea of darkness because she couldn't face herself and what she had lost, because she'd blamed herself. But it hadn't been her fault, no more than it was Mark's fault that his men had died.

They were simply human beings. Human beings who'd made mistakes. Human beings who'd found each other in spite of their imperfections.

Thanks to Mark, they had the rest of their lives to atone for those mistakes. And a future to look forward to together.

She gripped the tiny picture frame as she opened her

eyes. The blinding darkness she'd lived in all these months greeted her, then slowly faded. She blinked, the darkness blurring then a faint light gave way to Mark's handsome face, full of emotions, of love, of promises to keep.

And his eyes, they were that brilliant almond color with tiny slivers of yellow around the rims, just like sunshine.

Those eyes were filled with love and passion. And tears. She clutched the picture frame in one hand, then lifted the other toward him.

He caught her fingers in between his, a smile curving his mouth. "I can't believe it. You're all right." He hugged their joined hands to his heart. "I love you, Claire."

"I love you, too, Mark." She squeezed his fingers. "Your smile is the most beautiful thing I've ever seen."

His eyes widened. "You can see me?"

She nodded and reached up to touch his cheek. "Thank you for giving me back my life."

"Claire…" Mark said in a gruff whisper, "I want us to have that life together."

She wet her lips. "I want that, too."

He traced a finger along her jaw. "You won't mind being an FBI agent's wife?"

Tears filled her eyes. "I don't care what you do or where we live, Mark, as long as we're together."

Then he lowered his head and kissed her, the promises in his gentle touch a hint of everything they had to look forward to in the future. The cycle of love had been born again, giving them a second chance, the empty black slate now painted with the vibrancy of colors.

Claire intended to share the palette with him forever.

Epilogue

Claire's sister adjusted the train to Claire's wedding gown. "You look beautiful, Claire."

"I'm so glad you're here, Paulette. And I'm so grateful we had a chance to talk."

Paulette dabbed at her eyes with a tissue. "I can't believe you thought I had the perfect life when I've been so miserable this last year."

Claire hugged her sister, saddened that Paulette's marriage was ending when hers was just beginning. Paulette wanted to escape the confines of being the obedient, submissive wife and follow her own dreams for a change, instead of cowing to her dictator of a husband. Claire had had no idea how unhappy her sister had truly been. She'd been so caught up in her own tragedy that she'd been unaware of her sister's pain. Paulette had wanted Claire to live with her because Paulette had needed her as much as Claire had needed someone.

"I'm proud of you," Claire said. "It takes guts to do what you're doing."

"I have to admit I'm a little scared, but I'm also excited."

Claire lifted her sister's chin. "You're going to do great."

Paulette blushed, looking younger and happier than she had in years. "I have a good role model." The sisters hugged, both waving off tears as the wedding march began.

A few seconds later, Claire stood in front of the glowing candles, gazing into the eyes of the man she loved. A few of her friends at CIRP had arrived to celebrate with her, and Mark's best friend's wife and son sat amongst the guests. In the past three months, they had become a second family to both Mark and Claire. Mark had finally taken Kevin to see the Atlanta Braves play. In true fashion, Javier Lopez had hit a grand slam—Kevin had sworn his father had seen it in heaven. Mark had agreed.

Luke Devlin was Mark's best man. Paulette was her bridesmaid. She missed not having her father there to give her away, and vowed when she and Mark had a child, he or she wouldn't grow up without his.

At least that was what Mark had promised.

The preacher said a simple opening and prayer, then Mark took her hand in his.

"Claire, I fell in love with you the first moment I looked into your beautiful eyes. In them, I saw the soul mate I had been searching for. My lover, my friend, my life.

"But in the darkness of the past year, when I thought

I'd lost you and that light, I was lost myself." He squeezed her hand, his fingers caressing hers. "But today we stand here together, evidence that traveling through the tunnel of darkness is the way to see the light. And the love that brought us back together will shine forever."

Claire swallowed back tears, gripping his hand tightly. "The darkness that existed for you was a mere extension of myself, for you are right. You are my lover, my friend, my life. But I once was blinded by that darkness, clinging to the threads of forgotten dreams, until you took my hand and led me back. And in doing so, you restored my sight.

"There are all kinds of heroes in the world, men who fight for their country, for their honor, for their families, for their lives. You are all of those things and more, Mark. You've stood by your friends when they've fallen by your side, by their children when they are gone and by me when I needed you most. I love you now, tomorrow and always."

Without waiting for the reverend's permission, Mark dragged her into his arms and kissed her, sealing their vows with the tenderness and passion that Claire knew would carry them through the worst of storms and the sunniest of days.

Just as the reverend pronounced them man and wife, Mark swept her up against him and nuzzled her ear. Claire looped her arms around his neck and hugged him, kissing his mouth. Her wedding night loomed with all the possibilities of passion and romance and promises of tomorrow. It was a new beginning, a symbol of a long future together.

One in which they would create a new child and cement a love that would last forever.

* * * * *

If you liked Midnight Disclosures,
Be sure to pick up Rita Herron's next exciting book
THE MAN FROM FALCON RIDGE
Coming in November 2004
Only from Harlequin Intrigue

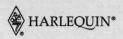

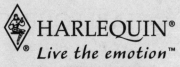

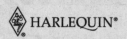

INTRIGUE®

and

B.J. DANIELS

invite you to join us for a trip to...

McCalls' Montana

Their land stretched for miles across
the Big Sky state...all of it hard earned—
none of it negotiable. Could family ties
withstand the weight of lasting legacy?

Starting in September 2004 look for:

THE COWGIRL
IN QUESTION

and

COWBOY ACCOMPLICE

**More books to follow
in the coming months.**

Available wherever Harlequin books are sold.

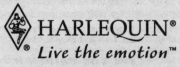

Live the emotion™

www.eHarlequin.com

HIMCCM

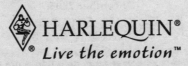

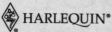